LOVE, LUST AND LIES

CATHLEEN ROSS

ISBN: 9798695918809

LOVE, LUST AND LIES

CATHLEEN ROSS

Feisty Gabriella Vitadini throws her husband Tony out when she finds out he is having an affair. Revenge sex with a hot, younger man feels good, except she misses her husband. Can Tony risk revealing his devastating secret to win her back?

ABOUT THE AUTHOR

Cathleen Ross likes to write about the quirky side of life. She loves writing romance featuring hot heroes and feisty heroines. When Cathleen's not writing for HarperCollins, she's working on her self-published novels.

To learn more, please visit
http://www.cathleenross.com
Email address for readers:
contact@cathleenross.com

ACKNOWLEDGMENTS

To my mother-in-law, Maria, and my dear father-in-law, Enore, for teaching me so much about Italian culture.

To Rob who taught me everything I know about love.

1

Once, when I nearly died, my husband said he couldn't live without me and, at the time, I believed him.

I came back from death for him.

When the doctor rushed me into hospital to have an emergency Caesarean, I couldn't see the doctor's scalpel but I could see the doctor's intense expression as he cut through my skin. I lay motionless behind the screen with the epidural in place, my husband Tony holding my hand.

Tony tried to rub warmth back into my hand, and I knew from his expression that every bit of energy he possessed was focused on me. 'It's going to be all right. They have a heartbeat. The baby is alive.'

I latched on to his words like an exhausted swimmer in need of a line. His voice calmed me the way it always did when life became too much.

He raised my fingers to his lips and kissed them. 'I'm here for you, Gabby.'

I clung to his hand. 'What if the baby dies?'

His face was bleached with exhaustion, but he was calm.

My rock in a storm- I always called him that.

'The baby has a strong heartbeat. Don't worry.' He put my hand to his cheek.

I squeezed my eyes shut and prayed for my baby's life. I prayed to God, I prayed to the blessed Virgin, I even prayed that my late mother would help me.

'We're pushing the baby's head back in the birth canal, so we can pull it out through your C-section,' the doctor said. 'You may feel some movement above your waistline.'

My whole body jolted. My eyes snapped open so that my gaze met Tony's. 'What's happening?' I cried.

'It's okay.' Tony stroked my hair. 'The baby's out. Don't worry.' He smiled as they held her up, but his smile died. His gaze shot to my face.

My body started to shake uncontrollably.

'Hold on, Gabby. Hold on,' he said.

I wanted to ask about my baby. I wanted to reach out for her, but I couldn't speak, couldn't will my arms to move.

'Heartbeat's low,' the doctor said.

I was so focused on the baby that it never occurred to me that the doctor was talking about me.

'We have to stem this bleeding.' There was no mistaking the urgency in the doctor's voice.

The world had taken on a different hue. The doctor seemed far away and the room had darkened around the edges until I could see no more. I was vaguely aware that Tony was by my side, but there was someone else there too.

Surrounded by white light, smiling at me, was my mother. Compelled by some unseen force, I went towards my mother, but then I looked back at Tony. There were tears streaming down his face.

'Come back, Gabby. Don't leave me,' he said, clutching my hand.

I saw the doctor shout to his assistant to get my husband out of the room, but Tony refused to budge.

How could I leave him when I loved him so much? And what of my dear little baby? I knew what it felt like to grow up motherless.

My mother held out her hand to me.

'I can't go,' I told her. 'Tony needs me. He can't look after our baby alone.'

When my mother faded from view, I realised I had been given a second chance.

I resisted the call of heaven because the bond between Tony and me was precious.

It's strange how life can change on the spin of a coin.

2

'You know, Christine, I've worked here two years now...' From my position behind the reception desk, I waved my TAFE Certificate in Real Estate in the air. 'And I'm finally certified.'

Certifiably crazy for trying to work full-time, raise a child, study late at night for two years, and maintain a happy marriage. Was that the reason Tony had strayed?

'I want to work on your sales team.'

In a rare moment when the phone was quiet at the end of the day, Christine Tolley, Manager of Martin Place Real Estate and the most driven boss in the world, stopped beside her office door and listened.

I held my breath waiting for her response.

'You'd like a place on my sales team?' Christine paused like the thought was totally new to her. Fortunately, she didn't frown, which meant either she was seriously considering the idea or she'd had a stab of Botox. I hoped it was the former.

Go-get-it Christine, with her sharp, blonde bob and body-moulding Dolce and Gabbana suits, never let anything stop her which is why she owned one of the most successful boutique real estate businesses in Sydney. I could learn from Christine.

I reconciled the accounts each month with Christine and I knew that the salesman who worked for Christine earned more in a week than I earned in a month. My jaw tensed as I waited for her answer. I had never defined myself by my work like many men do, but I truly loved real estate.

People didn't understand that selling a house is like an emotional tidal wave with enormous highs and rumbling lows. *I* knew it because I'd recently sold my Federation cottage on busy Military Road in Neutral Bay and bought a house nearby in a quiet corner of Cremorne. I'd been on such a high when we'd got our price. Maybe that's why real estate suited my temperament so well. After working in retail for many years I'd finally found a business I loved. 'You know you'll have to work Saturdays. What about Cami?'

I already worked full-time, so every moment with Cami was precious to me and Christine knew this. 'Tony will mind her.' To Cami, Dad was there for fun and games, I was there for hugs. She adored him. It was just me who wanted to sew shrimp shells in the hems of his trousers; snap off the heels of Betty-Big-Boob's shoes–yeah, well, you get the picture.

'He's good like that, your husband,' Christine said. 'He does anything for you. You're lucky to have him.'

'Yeah.' Christine didn't know about Tony's recent affair. I tried not to choke on my bile, but Christine was right about Tony. He was terrific around the house, once he got moving, and wonderful with Cami. But in bed? *Niente.* Nothing. I was invisible.

Christine walked over and stood by my desk, her long, painted nails tapping the surface. Her eyes narrowed and I detected a special gleam.

I knew that look. It meant she was calculating possible financial gain like I was some profit or loss statement.

Several relatives had listed their houses with Christine since

I'd joined, not that I'd made a cent out of the sales, but I was determined to change that.

'You're good with clients. Friendly. You look great and you're smart. I bet the male clients would go for a sexy little Italian like you.'

'Christine!'

She pointed at me with her pink manicured index finger. 'I'll take you on.' She turned on her Jimmy Choos and walked back to her office.

'Yes!' I wanted to leap up and kiss her, but that would muss her hair, and anyway, Aussies didn't kiss spontaneously like I did, with my Italian-Australian heritage. Instead I jumped up and down. 'Woo hoo!' I heard Christine laugh from her office.

I liked Christine. Really liked her. Culturally, we were miles apart. She didn't carry the migrant rules and regulations that seemed imbedded in me from my mother, like the Ten Commandments of which the eleventh, I was finding out, is– Thou shalt hold thy family together no matter how much thy husband cheats.

Finally, my career was coming together and I'd worked damn hard for it, having to prove myself all over again in a new area. If only Tony and I were like we were before I had Cami, before I got post-natal depression, my life would be perfect.

My heart thudded in my chest.

If only I could have that passion we once shared again.

I knew I had to move on, but the hole that lodged in my heart was a chasm of despair. It wasn't going to be easy to forget the love I had for Tony. Would I ever feel like that for someone else?

I closed my eyes and took a deep breath. Christine had survived a hideous divorce, but she had moved on.

I had to toughen up and get with the program like Christine.

Just as I put down the phone, the office door swung open.

Some serious dark-haired eye candy wearing a black leather jacket over an open-neck white shirt and tight black jeans strode into the office and up to my counter.

Hello. Handsome hunk alert. I sat up straight. I gave him my best, new salesperson, don't-show-the-braces smile.

I was aware of his height, over six feet, with wide shoulders like a football player, and narrow hips. I wanted to stare and stare and stare–

Wow. Hello? I was alive!

Despite evening approaching the man wore dark sunglasses, which he took off to reveal piercing green eyes.

My chin dropped. 'Can I help you?' I asked. I wished I'd had time to renew my lipstick. As it was, I'd just managed to put in my dental wax because the rough spots of my braces were chafing my gums.

'Hi. I'm Dave Angelo.'

'Gabriella Vitadini.' I held out my hand to shake his.

I don't know what happened when he took my hand. It was like my world stopped. Something sexual passed between us. I was sure I wasn't imagining it. It was like an electric charge passed through his palm to mine. Only it didn't stop there. I swear that charge went up my arm and exploded into all my erogenous zones. I didn't want to let his hand go.

'Pleased to meet you,' he said. He spoke with a deep voice and a slight accent that hinted at exotic places in Italy. Reaching inside his jacket, he pulled something out of his pocket.

I couldn't stop staring at him. *Va-va-boom!* This man was a god.

He took out a piece of paper, unfolded it, and placed it on the counter. I tried to drag my gaze away from his hands. They were large capable hands with raised sinews. My husband had petite accountant hands. Dave Angelo's hands looked like they belonged to a tradesman. Strong. Capable. Long fingers. I wondered what he did for a living.

I wondered what he could do with those powerful hands of his.

I decided not to slap my own face for my filthy thoughts.

'I want to see this one.' Dave pointed to one of the photographs. On the paper was our agency advertisement for the Temple–a block of luxury apartments just off Martin Place, with views of the harbour. Dave pointed at the penthouse–a four-million-dollar job with vaulted ceilings. The Temple also came with a pool, gym, sauna and plenty of marble.

With him standing so close I could smell leather and an aftershave that suggested summer in Taormina, Sicily. *Get a grip, Gabriella.*

I checked the office diary to see when our salesman Tony Benson would be back in the office. 'Our salesman is out right now. Would you like me to make an appointment tomorrow?'

A shadow of frustration crossed his features. 'I don't like to wait.'

I bet.

'Just a moment I'll talk to my boss and see if I can get you through ASAP.' In real estate, it's not smart to keep people waiting.

The stuttering click of Christine's approaching heels signalled that she'd nearly fallen over herself to get to Dave Angelo.

'Christine, this is Dave Angelo. Dave, this is our Company Director, Christine Tolley.' They shook hands and I swear I saw Christine shiver in delight. She smiled at him and her face lit up like sunlight.

'Mr Angelo wants to see the Temple penthouse.'

Christine looked at her watch and frowned. 'I have another appointment.'

Dave Angelo leaned on the counter and looked directly at me with those piercing eyes of his. 'You take me.'

Oh, yes, yes, yes!

'Good idea.' Christine smiled her always-please-the-client-and-get-his-money smile. She has very pointy eyeteeth; easy to imagine they could latch on to a wallet and never let go.

'Sure, show Mr Angelo through the Temple, Gabriella.' She walked behind my desk, opened a filing cabinet and pulled out the Temple contract. 'Get his signature,' she hissed.

I jumped up from my seat. 'Let's go then, before it gets dark,' I said to Dave.

He smiled and I took a deep breath. The man had perfect white teeth and the sort of smile that made me want to keep staring. 'Mmm.' His lips were full, the type of lips I could imagine kissing and kissing–

Christine nudged me.

I grabbed the Temple keys off the board and switched on the answering machine. I didn't look Christine in the eye. I didn't want her to think I could get flustered in front of a client, but there was something about the way that Dave looked at me that made me shivery with excitement.

'Bye, Christine,' I said.

'Bye, Gabriella.' Christine raised her fingers to her ear in a gesture that said '*phone me*'. I nodded.

I held open the door for Dave. 'It's a quick walk from here, though I'm sure you know that.'

Dave nodded, walked through the door, stopped, and held it so that I could let go and walk through. A gentleman. I liked that and I thanked him, but I kept my tone business-like because I suspected Dave was probably used to women swooning all over him. I was determined to be professional, especially now that I had made the sales team.

We strode into Martin Place which was noisy with the sound

of cars beeping their horns, along with taxis and buses. Grey-suited people jostled each other as they made their way home at the end of the day. I glanced at Dave who walked beside me. Everyone around me seemed rumpled and harried compared to Dave who walked with a confident gait. With his dark, shoulder-length hair, he didn't fit the businessman mould; his leather-clad look was more artisan, more free spirit.

'So where do you live?' I asked Dave, to get some conversation going and to escape my own neuroses.

There were a few other questions that I'd like to ask Dave — *Do you have a girlfriend? Are you married? What are you like in bed?*

'I'm staying in a hotel until I buy a place.'

Dave mentioned an upmarket hotel on Sydney Harbour not far from my office. 'Oh, that's nice. I had breakfast there once.'

Okay, I lie. I'd been a few times. When my husband stopped touching me, I didn't know what to do or how to win him back. I felt so unloved and I turned to food. *Stop thinking about yourself, Gabriella. Pay more attention to the client.* 'So, do you like your hotel?'

'Yes, Gabrrrriella, I like the hotel.'

I noticed that even though Dave had a slight Australian nasal sound mixed with his accent, his speech was formal, almost as if he was getting in touch with English again. I *loved* the way he said my name the Italian way, rolling the 'r', caressing it with his tongue. I had an image of him rolling his tongue over my nipples.

Oh God, stop it, Gabriella.

'The service is good,' Dave continued, 'but I need a place to stay when I'm in town,' he added. 'Business is increasing here.'

'So you're not local?' Talking gave me a good excuse to look at him. He had large eyes and a straight nose with slightly flared nostrils. I loved that he had high cheekbones that defined his face so that he looked masculine yet refined with it. And his mouth was to die for.

'I was born here, but I live in Florence. I left Australia when I was ten.'

'Florence, Italy? Wow! Lucky you, living there. There must be some great shoe buys there.'

'Gabrrrriella.'

I swear I shivered when he said that. I glanced up at him. He was frowning so that he looked serious, almost forbidding.

What had I said wrong?

'I deal in marble,' he said. His face lit up and he waved his hands to give his words emphasis. 'Florence is the great seat of art, of culture.'

'Oh. Yes. Of course. Art.' I tried to think of something intelligent to say about Italian artists. Shame hit me when I realised I could name many Italian shoe designers — Valleverde, Gucci, Salvatore Ferragamo, Prada — but was struggling to come up with the names of some artists. Fortunately, Dave Angelo smiled and winked at me.

'Italians are great craftsmen. Of course, my sisters love shoes more than galleries too.'

I laughed. I could see a twinkle in his eyes.

'But I as the man of the family have to concentrate on business. My family has a quarry in Northern Italy,' he added.

'A quarry?' *Gosh, a whole quarry.* 'You mean you import marble here?'

Dave nodded.

'So if I want a marble benchtop in my kitchen, I just have to talk to you?' Marble benchtop? Ha, ha, ha! A wave of panic gripped my chest. I haven't thought throught the repurcussions. With my broken marraige, I'd have to sell the house. Move Cami to another kindergarten. Oh God, I couldn't face what was ahead of me. I'd always thought that with Tony, our marriage would last. I realised in my misery that separated people always say that; the words had become no more than a cliché. I stepped off the curb. A taxi sounded its horn right near me. I jumped back.

'I can get you the very best,' Dave said.

I looked at him. He was so good on the eye that for a millisecond all my troubles disappeared. 'I bet. I mean, I'm sure you have a great product, er, great marbles...I mean marble.'

Dave laughed.

'*Mamma mia!*' I put my hand to my mouth then I started to giggle. I couldn't help it. My shoulders shook as I tried to suppress the laughter that bubbled up inside me. I looked away and caught sight of a reflection of a vivacious dark-haired woman, her eyes sparkling and...I stopped. It was my reflection.

Dave shook his head, but he still wore a smile from ear to ear like he could feel the electricity between us.

I skipped to catch up to him. Just being near him gave me pleasure. He moved so beautifully, his strides full of lion-like grace, his dark hair flowing like ribbons. I just wanted to look and look and look at him. It was surprising because I'd never gone for looks in the past, barely stared at other men, but back then I'd thought Tony was faithful to me.

'Er, what I meant to say is that great products help sell a place. My boss, Christine, says it's the woman who makes the decision about buying the house.'

'I agree. Italians say a woman makes a home.'

He gave me another blinding smile and the man was so damned gorgeous I nearly walked into a puddle.

'Careful.' Dave reached out and caught my arm to steady me.

'Thanks.' His touch sent tingles rocketing right up my arm to my nipples. He released me as soon as I was balanced, but I could still feel his fingers burn through my shirt sleeve like a hot coal.

We stopped at the lights on Elizabeth Street to cross the road. Men and women crowded either side of us. I could smell stale perfume. A Mercedes driver honked his horn as a cabbie stopped to let in a passenger without pulling over. Someone jostled me so that my arm bumped Dave's.

Dave looked around, his expression concerned. 'I'm sorry I got you out at such a busy time of day, Gabriella. My schedule is tight.'

'That's fine. Clients can't always make it in business hours. We're used to that at the agency.' I smiled. I couldn't help it. I was smiling so much my cheekbones ached. Dave was a momentary panacea to my wounds. There was something very likeable about him that went deeper than his looks. Italians have a word to describe things or people they like. *Simpatico.* It sort of translates to a mixture of nice and warm-hearted. After the shock of my husband's betrayal, I was desperately in need of kindness.

'So tell me. Gabriella is an Italian name. Where are your people from?'

The lights changed and we crossed the road. Dave's question didn't bother me the way it did when Tony's parents first asked it.

It's not unusual for people of Italian descent to ask this question. Sometimes, I think the Northerners do it to lord it over the Southerners, whom they consider beneath them. I know Tony's parents didn't like it that my parents came from Sicily. In fact, his mother had thanked God at the maternity ward that Cami had 'Northern' fair skin and not my *pelle scuro* dark skin. Even through my post-caesarean haze, I'd caught the insult. I'd nearly disconnected my drip needle and stuck it in her eye.

'My parents are both from Italy. Well, Mamma has passed away now. My father and my brothers live in Queensland.'

'You're lucky. It's wonderful to have family in the country,' Dave said. 'It's like I've left my heart at home. I feel lonely when I'm here.' He motioned to his chest, his hand balled into a fist.

'I get it.'

I knew where Dave was coming from. The family thing was ingrained in me from birth. I mentally stopped. Did I have a right to agree so confidently? After all, I was the one who threw Tony's cheating arse out of the family home, which meant I was the one breaking up the marriage. I was the one at fault. A divorced woman in my culture can still be considered a *disgrazia*. A disgrace.

The ridiculous thing was I knew I was living with values from the past. My brothers who have been recently to Italy told me it's not like that now among our generation, but the trouble was I was brought up with my parent's values from the last century and I hadn't moved on.

Getting rid of them was like liposuction–painful.

'So tell me, Gabriella, are you married?'

Was I? I thought about my wedding ring, which I'd ripped from my finger last night. I'd thrown it at Tony's retreating back. Bonk! It had hit him hard on the back of his head. He'd yelped and in a macabre sort of way his pain had given me a second of pleasure.

I took a deep breath. I looked at my feet and kept walking. 'I'm separated.' Oh hell, that made Dave the first person I had told. What would Dave think of me? Would he think I was a woman who couldn't hold my marriage together?

'It must have been your decision.' Dave stopped, turned, and looked into my eyes.

'W-what?' How did he know that? He gazed at me, the expression in his eyes intense.

'Stupid man. How could he let you go?'

'Huh? Why do you say that? You don't know me.' I was

vaguely aware that we were blocking the footpath. People pushed past us. I swear my heart was racing. My mouth dried.

Dave shrugged in an Italian way. 'It's what I think. You're beautiful. There's something very special about you.'

Was this Italian charm? I should know. I was from Italian descent but I was out of my depth.

'Would it worry you if I said I found you attractive, Gabrrrriella?'

Would it? Hell no!

'You remind me of a movie star. *Bellissima*.' He cupped both hands around my cheeks for a moment.

'You're kidding me, right?' Was my self-esteem so knocked apart I couldn't take a compliment?

'Gabrrrriella.'

'Oh! Um...right.' He thought I looked like a movie star. Had the man looked in the mirror lately? 'You're very Italian in the way you give compliments.' *Hot, flirtatious, charming.*

'You're very Australian in the way you receive them,' Dave laughed.

'I'm out of practice.'

He raised his eyebrow. 'I mean what I say, Gabrrrriella.'

Oh God, when he rolled his tongue like that I thought of the nipple-rolling thing.

My head was buzzing. I'd never felt so dazed and so good at the same time. I started walking fast and didn't stop until we reached the Temple.

I fished in my suit pocket for my keycard and inserted it into the Temple's glass entrance door. We stepped into the foyer area. I sorted through my keys avoiding Dave's gaze. I liked him all right, but was it appropriate to flirt with a client? 'The penthouse has its own private elevator.'

Oh, that was an exciting little tidbit of information. I inserted the key into the elevator slot. What happened to my

Italian charm when I needed it? Awkward. Tongue-tied. I needed to reconnect with my culture.

The elevator doors slid open and we walked inside. The elevator was cool and noiseless as it rose upward. I looked at the lift doors. I looked at the floor.

I touched my cheeks. Despite my olive skin, I'm sure they were pink. I could still feel Dave's touch on them. His stroke, sensuous and warm. His imprint.

Stop that, Gabriella!

When we entered into a large foyer, Dave's gaze swept over it. He bent to examine the tiles.

'*Bella*,' he said.

'The developer used the best finishes,' I agreed. 'Do you like the Carrara marble?'

'But it's limestone, Gabriella.' He gave me a quizzical look.

My insides curled. *Idiot!*

I could feel this sale slipping away. I didn't know my product. Christine would kill me.

'Don't worry, Gabrrrriella. People often mistake the two. Limestone is marble, but it is cut differently.' He hunkered down like a big prowling lion and tenderly stroked the limestone. 'See how the surface is slightly rough?'

I bent and felt it too. What else could I do? The man seemed genuinely interested in his stones and I was interested in his stones, too.

'Marble is smooth and soft. It is a clean stone with delicate veins like a woman's skin.'

His voice was hypnotising. Sensuous. Heat pooled between my thighs. I could see his attraction to me glinting in his eyes.

'Oh...um...yes.' I stroked the stone and my fingers tingled. 'Of course, it's limestone.' I laughed. 'I'm a bit short-sighted.'

Plop! Something came loose from my mouth.

I looked down. Oh God, a piece of wax had dislodged from my braces and fallen onto the stone.

Dave stared at it, sitting there like a large glob of spittle on the polished floor.

I swept it up. 'It's just wax.' My voice rose high. 'I need it for my braces on my teeth. It stops them cutting my gums.' Oh please. Could the Carrara, I mean limestone, just open up and swallow me?

My cheeks burned.

'Don't worry. That used to happen to one of my sisters who had braces. Your braces, they make you look–how do I say it–cute.'

He grinned and I immediately felt better, and yet, I was irritated too. Why couldn't I deal with Dave's Italian charm? Say something witty?

He motioned me in front of him. 'Come. Show me around.'

Off the foyer was a hall that led into an enormous living and dining area that had views all over the city. The sun had just set and I could see the lights of boats twinkling on the harbour. Both the Harbour Bridge and the Opera House were lit up.

'Fantastic,' Dave said.

'Best view of the harbour.'

I showed Dave through the rest of the apartment, noticing that he nodded in approval at the large master bedroom. I had an image of him lying on a bed naked, beckoning to me.

Maybe something like telepathy exists. Had I transmitted my sensual image? I have no idea, but at that moment Dave turned, and without saying a word, he took me in his arms and kissed me.

Professional that I am, I should have pushed him away. Instead, I kissed him back with the passion of a woman neglected by her husband. I clung to his shoulders and moulded my body to his so that my breasts pressed flat against his chest.

His chest, hard and firm against my softness, made my heart go thump, thump, thump.

Although my behaviour was wrong, my instincts were right. Dave could kiss. His lips were firm and possessive. His tongue intertwined with mine and he growled with such pleasure that a shiver of excitement shot through my body. Then his hand left the small of my back, grazed my shoulder, and slid down to my breast.

I knew then that things had gone too far, but the sensation of his thumb rubbing over my nipple blotted out every sensible thought in my mind.

My mobile phone rang and though I was aware of it, its urgent tone didn't penetrate the heady haze of my arousal.

Except, my mother instincts kicked in and I thought of Cami. What if my little girl needed me?

I tensed in Dave's arms.

It was getting late and the Catholic-guilt inside me took over. What if it was Christine wanting to know how the sale went? What if she called in to the Temple and found us like this? 'I-I have to get that. I have a little daughter at home.' I broke away from Dave and foraged in my handbag for my mobile phone.

My home number flashed up where Cami was waiting with Gia, Tony's cousin. Gia minded her after kindergarten finished, two days a week. The other days, Tony's mother, Daniella, had her. I was glad that I didn't have to face Daniella tonight.

Had Tony told her about us yet?

'Hello?'

'When are you coming home, Mamma?' Cami asked.

'Soon.'

'I don't feel well,' said her little voice.

'What's the matter?' My fingers tightened on the phone. I prayed Cami wasn't getting sick. A sick child was every working mother's dread. It was the time when mother-guilt hit me hardest even though Gia was an excellent carer. 'Let me speak to Gia, sweetie.'

'Is Cami sick, Gia?'

'Just a headache,' replied Gia. 'Would you like me to give her some paracetamol?'

'Take her temperature first. Only give it to her if she has one.'

I hung up on Gia. I knew if I ran fast I could manage to catch the bus to Cremorne, to get home to Cami.

'You have a child?' Dave asked.

'Yes. A little girl. She's not well.' While desire still coursed through my blood, my mother instincts took over.

'You must go to her,' he said.

I couldn't believe what I was hearing. I knew many men who would be pissed off because this clearly could have gone further.

'I hope you'll take me to see the apartment one more time before I make a decision.' I could see the way his lips curved into a smile. 'I think if I see this apartment again in the daylight I would very much like it.'

My head was spinning and I wanted to run my fingers over my lips to feel where he had just kissed me. 'I can make you an appointment first thing tomorrow. That's if you want me to take you?'

Dave's face was flushed and his green eyes glinted. 'I want you.'

I couldn't think of anything else except that I hadn't had enough of him. 'I need your details.'

Dave pulled an over-stuffed black leather wallet out of his pocket and sifted through it. He shook his head. 'I have my card here somewhere.' He pulled at his business card. Several credit cards and papers came loose and clattered on the floor.

'Crazy.' He laughed. 'Travel and a neat wallet don't mix.'

I bent and scooped up his cards, along with his passport, which lay open. 'Gorgeous photo.'

He smiled at my compliment, took back his cards and handed me his business card. 'You can reach me on this number, anytime. Day or night.'

When his fingertips touched mine the same electric shock of desire pulsed through them, but I barely noticed it. I was too busy looking at Dave's birth date on his passport.

Dave was twenty-nine.

3

When I hobbled in the door twenty minutes later, Cami shouted, 'Mamma!' and ran up the hall with arms outstretched. My dog, Bacci, who looked like a tampon, joined the fray, beating Cami down the hall, leaping around me, her string-like Spoodle tail wiggling in delight.

'Don't jump, Bacci,' I said, pushing the dog down, having already sacrificed my best pair of Victoria's Secret stockings to her claws. I dropped my handbag on the floor plus the heel of my shoe, which I'd snapped running after my bus at Wynyard. My shirt was sticking to my skin under my jacket. I'm sure I still had the glow of arousal on my face.

'Hello, Cami.' I studied my daughter's face while I shucked off the other shoe, then picked her up and put my hand on her forehead. She seemed cool. 'I thought you were sick.'

'Better now.' Her round little face broke out into a cheeky grin, so that she looked like her father when he was caught doing something wrong. I frowned at her.

'Cami! You weren't fooling, were you? I missed the bus so I caught a cab home to get here faster.'

Cami gave me the sweetest smile and hugged me tight. 'I missed you.'

She was playing me. I knew it and yet, there was something about my daughter's smile that caught my heart every time. Inside me, those old-fashioned values I couldn't shake felt a good Mamma should stay at home, but we needed the money I brought in since we'd bought the new house.

'I missed you too.' I hugged her back, trying to calm my mother-guilt. Cami's little fingers patted my face.

Why did we women take on so much? Did Tony feel guilty that he worked full-time? Of course not. Did he worry his child would turn out with emotional problems if he didn't spend enough time with her? Hey, he was home on weekends, reading the newspaper and watching footy on TV, wasn't he? Sure he helped around the house, but did he worry that he couldn't get on top of the household chores? Oh, don't make me laugh! Did he feel guilty when he was bonking Betty-Big-Boobs? Bastard!

Did I feel guilty about what had just happened with Dave? My head was still spinning. I'd barely had time to process it.

'You're here at last,' Gia said.

Ignoring the prickle of irritation I felt, I said, 'Hello'.

Gia walked up the hall, took her jacket off the hallstand and squeezed into it. A big girl, Gia only shopped vintage in order to find bargains, but she didn't seem to worry if they weren't in her size. She was smart, but seemed more focused on finding a husband than on her studies.

'What happened to you?' she asked, giving me the once over. 'You look all wet.'

'A taxi splashed me.'

Gia looked at her watch. 'You're a little later than usual.' She raised her eyebrows at me. 'You look flushed.'

I rubbed my cheek. It was heated. 'The salesman was out, so

I showed this client around one of the properties, then I rushed home in case Cami was sick.'

Gia's eyes narrowed as she sized me up. Did I mention that Gia has the ability of a sniffer dog? Except her expertise is not sniffing out drugs, but gossip. And our Italian community's gossip is not like normal gossip. Our gossip becomes the size of Jules Verne's octopus as opposed to a calamari. A thought struck me. Did Gia know about Tony? If so, did everyone know?

I had to be careful. I knew that if I talked about Dave Angelo, if I gave my client a name, my face would betray me.

I didn't want Gina to mention a guy's name to Tony who would mention it to his parents, who would tell all the relatives, who would tell all of Italian Sydney and I would become the *puttana* who had the affair that broke up the marriage.

Puttana translates to whore, but it also means prostitute. This might sound crazy, but I knew what could happen and I didn't want to go there. You have to remember, in Italian culture whatever goes wrong — it's always the woman's fault, ever since Eve tempted Adam.

'I should have rung you,' was all I said instead. I shifted Cami onto one hip, picked up my handbag and pulled out *Cosmopolitan* magazine, which I'd bought myself as a little pick-me-up treat. 'Here. I don't have any extra cash to make up for being late, but this is the latest *Cosmo*.' I'd been looking forward to reading my mag, but it's very hard to find someone to do the post-kindergarten to dinner timeslot, and I trusted Gia to do a great job with Cami.

'*Grazie*.' Gia smiled and snatched it up. '*Ciao*, Gabriella.'

'*Ciao*, Gia. Thank you for staying back.'

'Okay, Cami,' I said once Gia had left, 'it's time for a book and bed.' I walked down the hallway towards her bedroom.

'No!'

'Pardon?' I stared at her in surprise. 'What do you mean, no? You love books.'

'I want Dada to read to me.'

'Dada's not here.' My heart sank and the pain in my stomach etched like acid. I winced. I had to tell her the truth–her father had moved out. 'Cami, Dada's not living here any more. Dada and I have-' A key turned in the latch. We both looked expectantly at the door.

Tony walked in just like he did every evening. He put down his briefcase, took off his coat, and deposited it on the hallstand.

'Here he is, Mamma. Dada!' she squealed, reaching out to him.

He smiled at us. Smiled! Was the man delusional? Did my threat of castration mean nothing to him?

Tony strode down the hall and took Cami from me. '*Cara*,' he said, kissing her.

Ma che balle! I froze. I swear he was going to lose them. He looked at me and tried to kiss my cheek too, as if nothing had happened.

I jerked my face away.

'Don't you have somewhere to go?'

Tony looked at me. '*Ciao*, Gabriella.'

Ciao? Was that the best he could do? A friendly Italian hello? Didn't he realise that not only was I growing claws and fangs, I wanted to use them?

How typical of Tony to remain calm while I was fighting not to blow a fuse. At five foot seven, he wasn't much taller than I was, and unusually quiet for an Italian. After my noisy family of brothers, his quiet nature had been what attracted me to him in the first place. Ironic, isn't it, because I hate the way I can't get a response out of him when we fight.

I noticed his eyes were puffy and although he was immaculately turned out in his Zegna suit, blue silk Armani tie, and white Tommy Hilfiger shirt — all found for him by me in the January sales — he looked like he'd been hit by a truck.

'Read to me, Dada.' Cami patted his cheek to get his attention.

'Sure, honey.' He kissed Cami on the forehead. 'I'll put you to bed.'

'No!' I stamped my foot.

'Calm down, Gabriella.'

I really hated it when he said that to me.

'I want Dada to read to me,' Cami said. Her bottom lip turned out stubbornly like Tony's did and I felt like the two of them were against me. Ridiculous, I know. I was behaving like the child.

'Let me put Cami to bed. Then we need to talk,' he said.

'Argh!' Tony is so sickeningly sensible sometimes. Calm in the face of extreme danger. 'Do it quickly.'

Tony didn't flinch. The man always had courage. Damn him. He was going to need every bit of it when I was finished with him. My rock in the storm was about to experience a hurricane. I'd always loved his strength, but now it just made him seem impenetrable.

I clenched and unclenched my fingers until they ached. There was no way I was going to let Tony move back into the house as if nothing had ever happened. It was over.

Cami smiled and gave me a little wave. 'You look funny, Mamma. Your face is red.'

My gut tightened. I wasn't going to let Tony make me feel I was acting crazy. He'd gone too far.

Tony turned and carried Cami into her bedroom. Even his tread was light on the hall runner.

That was Tony. Quiet all over. He never even made a noise when he came, though he said it was because he'd trained himself to be silent through years of guilty masturbation.

How could someone be that controlled, that's what I want to know? How could a man born of Italian blood become so passionless? Why couldn't my husband beg my forgiveness and make love to me like he used to? I loved him so much it was painful, but I hated him too and it was the kernel of hatred that grew inside me, drawing on my need for revenge. I wasn't proud of that as it went against all of my Catholic church's teaching. Unfortunately, I wasn't good at forgiveness.

I thought of Dave Angelo and his passion. That was what I wanted. A man who felt things the way I did. A man who couldn't get enough of me, even though he was only twenty-nine - or maybe because he was only twenty-nine.

There was a knock at the door. Who the hell was this now? I thudded down the hall.

Bacci had her snout at the bottom of the door, her string-like tail was wagging which meant it was family.

I yanked open the door.

'*Buona Sera*, Gabriella.' My father-in-law, Pino, walked in and kissed me on the cheek. My mother-in-law, Daniella, followed closely behind him.'Daniella. Pino. Look, it's not a good time. Would you mind-'

'Nonna. Nonno.' Cami raced out of her bedroom and hugged her grandparents.

I watched the loving exchange. How was this break-up going to affect Cami? I bit my lip, worried a bit of dry skin until I ripped it off and tasted blood.

'Hi Mom. Hi Pa.' Tony followed Cami and kissed his parents. What was going on here? Tony was a strong man, but his strength came from the love his parents gave him, their wonderful support and belief in him. Although, as a wife, I had replaced them in importance, Tony was very close to his family.

But to ask them to come over now. Was he crazy?

'Cami needs to go to bed now.' Okay, so I sounded like a shrew.

'Of course,' said Pino. He reached out and patted my hand. Pino is a good man. Strong, sturdy, reliable, but I knew he would take his son's side on this. 'I see my son is putting Cami to bed.' *Meaning that I wasn't.*

'Nonna, come read to me with Dada.' Cami did a little skip of excitement at seeing her grandmother.

Pino walked into my lounge and sat while Daniella went into Cami's bedroom. Despite his archaic values, I normally got on well with my father-in-law. He often complimented me on my outfits and told anyone who would listen how well Cami was brought up.

He was tall, nearly six foot with thinning grey hair, a ruddy complexion and blue eyes, the colour of the Lago di Como from where he came. A retired engineer, he could spend dogged hours on one task until he got it right. A great cook, he always brought over a fresh bolognese sauce because Tony and Cami loved it.

When Cami suffered colic as a baby, Pino would lay her on his big stomach and she'd sleep. Cami adored her grandfather. All the above made me like him, but the concern I could see on his face would be for Tony.

My stomach burned and there was a rancid taste in my mouth.

'Look, Pino. This isn't a good time at the moment.'

Pino waved his hand for me to sit. '*Siediti*.'

Pino knew how to take control. When he was a boy during the war, the Germans lined up his father and uncles and shot them. After that horrifying experience, Pino, as the only surviving male, became the head of his family. He worked himself to the bone to help his mother support his younger siblings and his word became law from a young age.

My leather lounge made a poofing sound as I sat.

'My son tells me you have asked him to leave.' He leaned forward so that his stomach squashed over his belt.

'Look, Pino, I don't want to talk about this with you right now.'

Pino waved his hand at me as if my obduracy didn't affect him. 'You listen, Gabriella.'

Bacci wagged her tail and put her head on Pino's knee.

'When I was a boy, the priest in our village betrayed the men of my family to the Germans, for hiding Partisans. I lost my faith in God that day, but I believe in one thing. Family,' my father-in-law continued. 'Tony has been very stupid.'

Translation: Tony got caught.

'Stupid?' my voice rose as anger bubbled in my chest. I hadn't lost loved ones in the war like Pino, but I had a war in my heart. I understood the knife of betrayal. 'Tony's having an affair!'

'Gabriella, this is a marriage.'

Translation: You should put up with the affair. It's part of the deal.

His viewpoint didn't surprise me because in one embittered moment Daniella had told me of Pino's infidelities.

'You can't throw Tony out over another woman.'

Translation: You should turn a blind eye.

I folded my arms in front of me. 'I said...he's having an affair.'

'What about Cami? How can you make her suffer? Look how happy she is. You gonna spoil that?'

Translation: You're a bad mother if you put yourself before marriage and family.

Pino knew the way to my heart. I wondered if he had worked the mother-guilt angle on Daniella when he had been caught cheating when Tony was younger.

'Tony and I will work out access so Cami doesn't suffer. He's still her father. That doesn't change.'

Pino shrugged. 'I don't understand.'

Translation: Why didn't I agree with him?

'You've been together a long time. Why can't you do the Italian Marriage? You stay together. Tony does what he wants and you do what you want.'

Translation: Tony does what he wants and you do what Tony wants.

'I don't want the Italian Marriage. I want a husband who loves me. A man who is faithful.'

Just then Tony and Daniella came into the sitting room.

I rose to my feet before Daniella and Tony had a chance to make themselves comfortable on the lounge. There was no way I was going to let all three of them put me on trial. Daniella, despite her suffering over Pino's infidelities, would take her husband's side. No doubt her role as a wife and mother had been ingrained in her from her mother.

Daniella's father had a secret illegitimate son to a village woman, but he had paid to send her and the baby away. Daniella approved of this action. Her mother hadn't left or tossed him out because that would have been a disgrace. Instead, her mother had put up with the infidelity, just as Daniella had. 'Please, Pino. Daniella. Tony and I need to talk, alone.'

Pino stood. 'Remember, Gabriella. We are your family.'

'Mom. Pa. Leave this to me.' Tony turned and tried to usher them down the hall, but Daniella wasn't having a bar of it.

'I have something to say.' She waved her hand to silence Tony.

Daniella at five foot five wore enough gold to decorate a Christmas tree, but it looked good on her because she knew how to team her accessories with Versace and Armani. She was very stylish and looked younger than her sixty-five years.

I was grateful to her because she minded Cami so I could work. I figured she saved me years of mother-guilt because I never worried when she had Cami. She was also very generous to me, not taking a cent for all the child-minding. I loved my mother-in-law, but I knew in her eyes Tony could do no wrong, which would lay the blame for any marital problems at my door. Perhaps that sounded clichéd, but I've yet to meet an Italian mother in my circle that doesn't blame the daughter-in-law for whatever goes wrong in a marriage.

'You told my son to leave,' Daniella said, her hazel eyes glowing. 'He came to me like a dog in the night. I couldn't believe it, Gabriella. How could you? My son. Homeless.'

'You went to your parents?' I stared at Tony. I couldn't believe that. Here I was imagining him cosily ensconced with Betty-Big-Boobs.

'Of course,' Tony said.

'What's the matter? Doesn't Betty cook?'

'I had to give you time to cool down.' There was a look of appeal in Tony's eyes, but that wasn't enough for me. I needed words. I needed him to beg my forgiveness. I needed to know that he would never do it again.

'You can't throw our marriage away over one affair.'

Translation: Forgive this affair and all the ones that follow.

It was the certainty of Tony's tone that got me. Sure there was appeal, but there was no contrition in his eyes. No shame. He expected me to forgive him. Expected it just like Pino expected Daniella to put up with whatever he did.

I gritted my teeth.

I looked at Pino who was nodding his head like a wise old man who had seen worse things in his life and survived them. 'You need to calm down, Gabriella.'

Translation: Your Southern Italian emotions are getting the better of you.

Tony showed his parents out. While he did that I checked on Cami, admired our beautiful, sleeping daughter who we had made together in a time when we had been happy. How had that happiness disappeared like smoke in the wind? Surely, after so many years together we'd made better foundations, or had

Tony been playing around all along and I'd been none the wiser?

Tony joined me at the door of our daughter's bedroom.

'What would change if you came back?' My voice was quiet. I turned to him.

'What do you mean?'

'Exactly what I asked. How will *you* be different?' Waves of pain assaulted me. *I knew I would never feel the same. Did he really think he could come back without making any effort to win my forgiveness?*

Tony looked confused. 'I won't be different.'

That was what I thought. 'I'm not willing to settle for the Italian Marriage. I want you to love me.'

'I do love you, Gabby. You're the mother of my child.'

'Oh yes, the Madonna.' Why did the whore have to be the one to get all the fun? Tony tried to take my hand. I jerked my hand out of his reach.

'Look Gabby, it's going to take time.'

How had my husband become so unfeeling? 'I want to know why you had an affair.'

'It was just sex.' Tony shrugged. There was almost an expression of bewilderment on his face as if he didn't know himself.

'But why did you do it? Why won't you have sex with me? What is wrong with me?'

Tony looked away unable to meet my gaze.

'I hate the way you won't talk to me about our sex life.' I persisted. 'Have you ever been faithful to me?'

'Of course. I–' Tony protested, but I cut him off.

'Your infidelity destroyed me,' I said, my voice emotional. 'It means I can't trust you. It means that every time you're late, I'll think you're with her. It means that every time the phone rings and I hear you speaking quietly, I'll think it's her. I don't want to live like that. I'm not going to accept the Italian Marriage. That's not good enough for me. I'm not going to accept not having a sex life any more.' I pushed past him into our bedroom and yanked out a suitcase from under the bed. Flinging it open, I stuffed it full of his clothes.

Tony followed me, his face creased with concern. 'Gabby, stop being crazy.'

I rounded on him. 'I'm always the crazy one. The *pazzo* wife who went to the clinic after giving birth. The one they put away with post-natal depression. Whatever you do to me, I'm the crazy one.'

'Shush. I know you're not crazy. It wasn't your fault you were sick. Please don't start screaming again. You'll wake Cami.'

'I'll show you crazy,' I said, ignoring his appeal. I stormed out of our bedroom and returned with a pair of sharp scissors.

Tony's eyes widened in alarm. 'Gabriella!'

'This is crazy.' I waved the scissors in the air. I drove my arm down stabbing the scissors into Tony's best suit, which sat on top of his bundle of clothes in the suitcase. Right into the crotch. Tony jumped like I'd stabbed him.

I raised the scissors high to stab at his clothes again.

'*Basta,* Gabriella,' Tony cried. 'Stop.'

I stopped. 'Go!' I flung the scissors across the room so that they smashed against the wall.

He grabbed the suitcase and pushed it shut so that the clothes were squashing out of the sides.

I'd cut him where it hurt. A one thousand dollar Versace suit ruined.

I pushed past him and threw open the front door. 'Go back to your parents and their Italian Marriage.'

Tony's face was bleached like it was the night I'd almost died. Only this time, instead of fighting to stay together, I was fighting to destroy us.

'Stop screaming. We have to talk sensibly.'

That did it for me. A fuse went BOOM in my head.

'This is not screaming. THIS IS SCREAMING. GO! GO! GO!' My ancestors living under Mount Etna would have been proud of me. I yelled so loud in his face that he stepped backwards and nearly fell down the front stairs. Even Bacci who normally loved noise had fled to the other end of the house.

Tony left, trailing clothes behind him, a thin figure with a battered suitcase.

Did I feel remorse? Are you kidding? I was empowered. I had been starved of sex for three years while my husband was off screwing someone else. I wasn't going to take it any more. I had Dave, and even if it didn't last more than a day, I knew I was a sexually desirable woman.

I couldn't wait any longer.

4

I did something unusual after I threw Tony out. I decided to put myself first. I decided to put myself on the 'to be looked after' high priority list.

In my new state of selfish woman, I took special care with my appearance when I got up at six that morning. I washed my hair. I lashed on my extra-firming concentrate to disguise the slightly loose skin around my throat area. Then I outlined my eyes with black eye pencil and applied lots of mascara. I was going to see Dave Angelo that morning and I could barely contain my excitement.

I knew Dave was way too young. A totally unsuitable prospect for me. That didn't stop me tingling at the thought of seeing him. I guess my forty-year-old brain wasn't listening to my love-starved body. I had unfinished business with Dave. I put on a silky moss-green camisole under my suit and teamed it with sheer stockings. I made sure I had on my best sheer black underwear that I normally wore on special occasions. I knew Dave would like this look.

Cami came into the bathroom holding her teddy bear in one hand and sucking her thumb on the other. 'Where's Dada?'

'He's staying with Nonna and Nonno.'

'Coming back now?'

'Today is your day with Nonna, so if we leave early, you can see him before he goes to work,' I said, avoiding answering the question.

Cami dropped her bear and clapped her hands together, her delight in direct disproportion to how I felt.

'Come. You can have *biscotti* and latte for breakfast as a special treat.'

'Biscuits? Milk?' Cami's almond-shaped eyes widened. She knew I was fussy about what she ate. Our breakfast usually consisted of toast and fruit.

'And this morning you can dip the biscuits in the milk like Nonno does.'

Cami beamed.

I never said I was above using distraction and a bit of bribery in raising children.

Tony's parents lived around the corner on Rangers Road,and Daniella answered the door when I dropped off Cami.

I didn't know whether to kiss her cheek. Would she hate me now that I wouldn't have Tony's cheating arse back? After all, she had put up with Pino's cheating all her life. I knew she saw it as her role to hold the family together, which she did very well. Daniella solved the problem by kissing me on both cheeks, and Cami, too.

Still in her nightgown, which was unusual for her, Daniella waved Tony's shirt at me. 'Tony's so unhappy, Gabriella.'

No matter what Tony did to me, he would always be in the right with his mother.

'I know he never says he's sorry. He's like Bisnonna's

husband. God rest his soul.' She crossed herself looking upwards. 'But please take him back.'

Daniella believed all her late relatives were looking down on her from heaven- as if we women didn't have enough loved ones judging us here on earth.

I heard a shuffling step. I glanced behind her. Tony was nowhere to be seen, but old Bisnonna shuffled by minus her wig. She glared at me. Thin wisps of grey hair stood up on her head. Her eyes were puffy, her eyelids having long ago lost their eyelashes. I shivered. It didn't matter how frail she seemed, I was scared of Daniella's mother because she had the Evil Eye.

Old Bisnonna had hated her husband. From a bad family, he had told the town that he had been with her. She had been forced to marry him by her shamed parents. That man had died a slow cancerous death with old Bisnonna watching over him. She had played the role of the long-suffering, martyred Italian wife with a twist as sharp as a knife's blade.

Everyone was scared of old Bisnonna, except Daniella and Tony. But they were safe in the knowledge that she loved them. Unlike me.

Already, I'd suffered multiple miscarriages and post-natal depression. Would I get cancer next? Was my whole way of thinking ridiculous? Of course it was. I might be Australian but I wasn't able to escape from my cultural beliefs.

Old Bisnonna walked toward me, pointing her finger. My jaw tensed. I ground my teeth as she approached.

'I look after my husband. I no complain.'

Her pointed finger started shaking. Oh shit! Was she going to curse me?

Daniella turned to her mother. '*Basta*! Your husband gambled all your inheritance. We had nothing as children. We had to put bait on the windowsill to catch pigeons to eat when he lost everything. You didn't complain. Maybe you should have.'

Daniella crossed herself, glancing heavenwards.

I watched as Bisnonna muttered something and shuffled from the hall. I'd never heard Daniella snap at her mother. No matter how often old Bisnonna disappeared onto the street in her nightgown, Daniella never lost it.

Cami, sensing her grandmother's mood, reached out and patted her hand. Daniella bent and cuddled her. I noticed dark shadows under her eyes.

'*Cara*,' she crooned.

I bent and kissed Cami goodbye. 'I have to go to work but I need you to help your grandmother today. Make sure Bisnonna doesn't go wandering. If she tries to leave the home, you run and tell Nonna.'

'Are you sure you're okay to have Cami?' I asked Daniella when Cami had gone. Was it fair that Daniella got stuck with my husband, her aging demented mother, Pino, and Cami too?

Daniella paled. 'You wouldn't stop me seeing Cami?'

For a moment my elegant mother-in-law's face was stripped of composure.

Did she see me as the enemy now?

'No! I'd never take Cami from you. You've helped me so much. Because of you, I can work. It's just that you look harassed this morning.'

Daniella threw up her hands. 'I have two of them to look after now. One complains his minestrone has too much salt. The other not enough. All I ask is that they keep an eye on Bisnonna while I'm clearing up dinner. But can they do that? I ask you?'

'What happened?'

'The Police found her walking down the street.'

I patted her on the arm. 'Don't worry. It's not the first time.'

Daniella leaned forward so that I could feel her breath on my face. 'She was *nuda*. *Nuda*!'

'Naked? What? Not even her nightgown?' Sheesh! Not a good look there. 'How embarrassing.'

'She drink Pino's wine. It make her crazy.'

'You're lucky she didn't get hit by a car,' I said.

Daniella leaned forward. 'Officer Pantorelli found her. You think he won't tell his mother?'

Mrs Pantorelli was Daniella's nemesis since Tony had broken off his engagement to her daughter twenty-one years ago. Mrs Pantorelli said her daughter was 'soiled goods' and that Tony should have married her. Personally, I think her daughter had a lucky escape.

'I don't know what you can do about Bisnonna.' Actually, I did. There was a good home with a lock-up facility on Awarba Street, but Daniella wouldn't hear of her mother going into a home. To do so would be a disgrace, plus Daniella would become the subject of gossip among her community.

'You think I can trust Pino and Tony to keep an eye on her? How can I get my shopping done?'

Okay. I admit it. I was feeling guilty now. Not that it was hard to make a convent-raised girl feel guilty. We were fed on guilt morning, noon and night. Was that why I was so culturally obedient and yet resentful at the same time?

So I found myself swapping one torture for another. I offered to take old Bisnonna on Sunday to give Daniella a break. I figured that taking nutty, naked Bisnonna with the Evil Eye was a fair trade for Daniella having Tony back.

5

When I arrived at work, I found the divine Dave Angelo waiting for me. I don't know if he got better looking overnight, but he sure seemed it to me. Was it the combination of his dark shoulder-length curls and green eyes? Or the way he was dressed, so stylishly? Or, perhaps, the way he stared at me with the intensity men usually reserve for exotic sports cars and raunchily-clad women.

Pa-Boom...my heart missed a beat.

Dave was wearing a three-quarter, chocolate leather coat, with a round-neck T-shirt underneath that was a shade darker than the coat. In the business centre of the city most men wore identity-killing grey suits, so Dave looked sexily distinguished from the top of his head to his loafer-clad feet.

Christine stood next to him but, I confess, I'd barely noticed my boss. 'Good morning,' I said to both of them, not taking my eyes off Dave.

A tingling feeling that had started at the base of my spine was working its way upwards. I couldn't wait to get him to myself.

He smiled, reached out and took my hand.

I don't think I remembered to shake his hand. I was aware of the warmth of his touch, the way his hand felt in mine. I remembered how it had felt on my breast. Already, I could feel my cheeks glowing.

'Good morning, Gabriella.' Christine opened her eyes wide and stared pointedly at my hand that was still in Dave's.

I jerked it back and looked at my watch to hide my embarrassment. It was eight-thirty, half an hour before our appointment. 'Dave. You beat me in. You must be keen to see the Temple again.'

'Gabrrrriella. I am–how do you say it–excited.' His mouth broke into a slow smile.

Yup. That just about did it for me. It was all good. The intense look he gave me nearly knocked me off my Manolos, bought in this year's department store sale.

I suddenly remembered that I hadn't called Christine last night to tell her how the inspection went, as I was somewhat preoccupied with stabbing Tony's Versace suit. Was she angry with me? It was hard to tell with Christine. Unlike me, she was good at keeping her feelings to herself.

'I'm sorry I didn't get a chance to call you,' I said to my boss.

'Not a problem. Take Mr Angelo back to the Temple.' Christine smiled. 'He obviously likes it.' I could see her eyeteeth gleaming and knew I was in the clear. Christine could smell a potential sale the way I could smell the calories off a pizza.

'Let's get going then.' I nodded to Dave. I opened the door for him.

'So Gabrrrriella.' Dave smiled.

Did he really have to purr my name?

'Dave?'

'How was your little girl?'

'Cami?'

'She was unwell?'

How nice of him to ask considering what he had missed out on because of Cami's call.'Cami was fine. She just wanted me home.'

'I like children. I hope to have many, one day.'

Oh. Scary. That certainly wasn't an aspiration I shared considering the trouble I had been through. 'So what do you like doing in your spare time?' I asked, to change the subject.

'I love rockclimbing in the Dolomiti in summer and skiing there in the winter.'

Oh my God, I couldn't even lift my mum bum off the ground, let alone rockclimb. The only sport I liked was hunting shoes. I detested it when Tony watched endless footy games on television. I glanced sideways at Dave. I could find uses for a man with a body like that.

As Dave walked beside me, his hand kept brushing mine. I could feel the little hairs on his hands touching mine. A shiver passed up my arm. I was supposed to be selling him an apartment, but I couldn't stop thinking about sex.

When we arrived at the Temple, we took the elevator up to the penthouse. 'It's good this time of morning. You'll get to see the apartment in daylight.'

Dave stood close beside me, so that his leather jacket brushed my arm. I could smell his cologne, a mixture of spice and wood scent. The elevator door opened and we stepped out into the foyer and then the spacious living area.

'I already know I want it, Gabriella. It is *bellissima*.'

'You do?'

'*Si*. I've looked already at many new apartments. This one is the best, no?'

I couldn't believe it. There was a sale in front of me. My first sale!

But Dave wasn't looking at the view of the harbour. Instead, he stood kissing distance away, looking straight into my eyes. 'I want you in it. Last night I couldn't sleep.'

My throat went dry. Dave bent and kissed me.

And what did I do?

I wrapped my arms around him like a woman starved of affection. Could I eradicate Tony from my life by being with Dave? I didn't know, but I wanted to try. I should have been thinking about my sale, but Dave's body was hard and lean and I so desperately wanted him inside of me. What woman wouldn't want a man like Dave devoted to her?

Dave moved from my lips to my throat. He pushed my jacket off so that it fell onto the carpeted floor. I could feel my nipples tingling. What would it be like to have his lips on my breasts?

'Very nice,' he said appreciatively as he eyed my sexy camisole. He ran his hands over my breasts, holding his palm flat where my nipples peaked.

'You have the most fantastic breasts I have ever seen. Full. Beautiful.'

There was something about the level of his appreciation that helped me get over my lack of confidence about my body. I wasn't physically perfect like him, but Dave didn't seem to care. I wasn't used to such enthusiasm.

I slipped the camisole over my head because I knew that he would enjoy the sight of my sheer black bra, which matched my underwear. My nipples were pointy and aching to be sucked.

'Take the skirt off, too. I want to see all of you.'

I obliged so I was standing there in my sheer underwear, stockings and stilettos.

'Go. Walk over to the kitchen bench and bend over,' he ordered.

I stared at him. This was a side of him I hadn't seen before. Every nerve ending in my body was on fire for him.

'Spread your legs wide,' he ordered. 'Don't move.'

It was strange the way he ordered me about and yet, it was erotic too. He was still fully clothed and he walked up close surveying every inch of me.

Occasionally his hand would graze over me, sending little ripples of pleasure over my expectant skin.

I wondered what he was going to do to me. Was he going to take off his clothes? God knows, I ached for him. My clitoris was already throbbing.

'Face ahead,' he ordered.

I don't know why he didn't want me to look at him, but I didn't care. It made it more exciting for me, wondering what he was about to do as he stood directly behind me, smelling of his leather jacket and cologne.

'I love this underwear,' he growled in my ear.

He slid one finger under my panties directly into my slit, sliding it forward until he found my clitoris. I bucked to meet his finger. I wanted to rub against it, searching for the sensation I'd experienced last night.

'Don't move,' he said again. 'I want you to do everything I say.'

I knew he was controlling then, but I didn't know if that was the way he liked his sex or that was his whole character. Perhaps I should have walked out. Perhaps I should have stopped him, but I was hot for his caress. He slid another finger into my slit and used the other hand to stroke my nipples through my sheer bra.

I gasped at the double sensation.

'Don't move. See how long you can last as I pleasure you.'

Ha! This was his game. Torture and tease. God he was good at it. I tried not to move as he fingers slid up and down over my well-oiled slit, but it wasn't easy.

'Do you like this?' he asked, leaning close to my ear.

'Of course I do.' My legs started to tremble. Already I could feel little waves of pleasure starting in the base of my spine. If he kept strumming me like that I would come. I didn't know how he had so much self-control.

Dave flipped me over and lay me back on the marble benchtop like I was a delicious platter about to be devoured. He pulled my sheer panties aside and licked me all over, every fold, every crease.

I bucked my hips to meet his tongue. I was hot and squirming, but Dave pressed my hips so that I couldn't writhe uncontrollably like I wanted.

I needed to move because I wanted to come. How could I not? He was eating me like gelato. He licked over my clitoris but refused to let me raise my hips to meet him.

'Please, Dave,' I begged him. 'I need to come.'

But Dave just kept on licking me and pressing my hips down, so that I couldn't get the angle quite right. I tried to keep still and focus on my breathing. In. Out. In. Out. I tightened my lower abdominal muscles, so that I could subtly raise my pelvis by sucking in my tummy muscles.

I came with such a rush I couldn't contain my moans of pleasure.

Eyes closed, legs still spread, I heard a zipping noise and saw Dave undo his fly. *Finally*. He pulled out his weighty cock, which I saw had a big head on it, and pulled on a condom.

Without missing a beat he slid into me.

'I've been thinking about this all night,' he repeated.

I'd been thinking about this for three years.

Dave was hard and big and I couldn't believe how fantastic he felt. This time when I bucked to meet him he didn't order me not to move. Instead, he seemed to be enjoying my enthusiasm.

He leaned over me, pulled my bra aside and licked my nipples. I came again. He was deep inside of me and licking my sensitive peaks at the same time. I couldn't contain my delight.

With a deep groan Dave gave one last shove and shuddered.

'That was fantastic, Gabrrrrriella,' he said. 'I like it that you're obedient.'

'Yeah, well, don't get used to it, because it's not my style unless it suits me.'

Dave chuckled.

He pulled out of me, but as he did so, he reached over to my hips and pulled off my underwear.

'Hey, what are you doing?' I was suddenly aware that I was nearly naked and Dave was clothed. I watched as he tucked them into his pocket, part of them hanging out like a handkerchief.

'A memento,' he said. 'When I am not with you, I still have a part of you.'

Did this mean he wanted to see me again or was he some kind of memento weirdo?

Dave reached out and helped me off the kitchen counter. He watched as I dressed, a satisfied smile on his handsome face.

'We celebrate the sale. Yes? Dinner. Saturday night.'

I couldn't believe it. A sale and a date. Dave wanted to see me again. He didn't think I was some kind of slut because I'd slept with him so soon. Instead, he seemed to enjoy my sexuality.

It had been a long time since a man had celebrated my love of sex.

6

Tony rang me at work and I agreed to meet him in a coffee shop on Macquarie Street; the busy one that sold aromatic coffee and pizza.

We needed to talk. I knew that. Although I tried to hold on tight to my emotions, I couldn't trust that my anger wouldn't flare suddenly like Mount Etna. So I guess the coffee shop was a safe place for both of us.

There were so many things I still wanted to know. I needed to know why he had cheated on me. I couldn't leave it alone. But more than that, I wanted to see contrition in his eyes. I wanted to see the pain he had caused me, reflected in his eyes. I wanted to hear him say he was wrong. Without that, I knew I could never rid myself of the anger that burned deep inside.

Tony agreed to leave his work to come and meet me, which was a first. There had been a seismic shift in the power base of our relationship. Tony was no longer the man of the house. It was funny that I made most of the decisions in regard to running the house and Cami's upbringing, yet I had still thought of him as *Il Capo*. The boss. Now I had to work out an arrangement so he could see Cami on a regular basis; I didn't think of him as being in charge any more. That knowledge, combined with the success of my sale, not to mention my sex life, gave me the shot in the arm that I needed.

I'd always been accountable to men - first my father and then Tony. I'd never had a period in my life where I hadn't been accountable to a male.It seems absurd for a woman living in Australia, but in my culture it wasn't so unusual. The man was considered to be the boss of the family. That doesn't mean I was a wimp and did everything I was told. Of course I didn't. I was too fiery for that.

With my father, we'd suffered so much losing Mamma that I didn't want to hurt him. With Tony, I believed in my marriage, so although we'd had our disagreements over our sex life, I'd thought he was a good man and I'd tried hard to make him happy.

I pushed past the crowd on the footpath that was waiting for the bus. I paused at the glass doorway of the café, scanning the room for Tony. I almost didn't recognise him sitting hunched by the window, his hand clutching his short black as if he were cold. He seemed small.

As I approached, I noticed his face was pale, tinged with grey. The skin where he shaved looked reddened as if he were allergic to his shaving cream. He'd lost that king-of-the-world look that cosseted men often wear.

'Gabriella.' Tony stood and tried to kiss me in greeting.

I dodged him and slid into the seat opposite. The thought of giving the polite Italian customary greeting of a kiss on his cheek, was abhorrent. 'Tony.'

'Do you want something?' He pushed the menu over to me but I didn't bother to look at it. My stomach clenched as anger roiled. Once I'd made the decision to let him go, I wanted payback. I wasn't happy about my feelings, but I couldn't put them aside either. Some of my friends managed to maintain a friendship after they separated, but I'd never understood that. Once someone was gone from my heart that was it. I never wanted to see them again.

'A coffee.'

Tony called the waitress and proceeded to order for me.

'A cappuccino, please,' I interjected.

Tony's face registered surprise, but he didn't say anything. 'So how have you been?' he asked, when the waitress had left.

'Great.'

I saw him start at that.

I looked into his eyes wondering how this man I had loved for so long could betray me. His hazel eyes were dark with misery. Did that move me? Not at all. Revenge sat in my heart. I wasn't proud of that, but I was human and couldn't help it.

I felt nothing when I looked at him. There was a weird empty feeling where my heart beat in my chest. I didn't bother asking him how he was.

'I want to talk about your access to Cami,' I said.

'Please, Gabriella.' Tony leaned forward. He reached across the table to take my hand but I placed my hand in my lap. Tony's remained on the white Formica tabletop like a pale starfish washed up on the sand. 'We have to talk about us.'

I waited.

'I can't stay at my parents forever. You have no idea what it's like. Bisnonna's following me around the house. I can't get a moment's peace. Mum's mad at me. She says I'm like Pino.'

'A philanderer, you mean?'

Tony's mouth tightened.

'And what does Pino say?'

'He says I'm stupid.'

'Really?'

Tony nodded.

Then I thought about it from Pino's perspective. 'Stupid to do it or stupid because you got caught?'

Tony's mouth tightened again.

The waitress arrived with my cappuccino. I ripped off the end of a straw of sugar, dumped it in the cup, and stirred. The froth seethed over the side of the cup.

'Why don't you go live with Betty?'

Tony started.

He waved his hand. 'It's over.'

'Why? Isn't cheating fun any more? You're free now. Bonk the whole damn world for all I care.'

'Gabby, I'm a family man. I belong with you and Cami.'

There's something bizarre about betrayal. The person who does it just doesn't get how painful it is for the betrayed. Worse still, since Tony wouldn't discuss why he wouldn't have sex with me, no matter how much I badgered him, the problem never went away.

Italian men pride themselves on their virility and I, as an Italian-Australian wife, expected to get the goods.

'Please, Gabby,' Tony continued. 'Betty. It meant nothing.'

Blink! On went the light bulb. Quite clearly, Tony wasn't emotionally involved with Betty-Big-Boobs. I bet to Tony's way of thinking, his affair wasn't infidelity.

Daniella had once told me that Pino considered the women he had on the side as no more than *puttana*, sluts. She knew he'd never leave her for them.

Did it ever occur to her to leave?

I went in for the kill. 'What was Betty? Someone to scratch an itch?'

I watched as Tony shifted in his chair watching me warily. He withdrew his hand from the table and folded his arms.

I had no mercy.

'How does Betty feel? What did the affair mean to her? How

long did the affair go on? Is she hurt the way I am?'

I could see the discomfort on Tony's face.

'*Basta*,' he said.

I slapped my hand on the table. 'I will say when it's enough. You damn well owe me an explanation. You better explain to me why you haven't had sex with me in three years, went screwing someone else, and then think I'll have you back.' I stared at him. Waiting.

'I-I can't explain about you and me.' Tony looked hunched over and sick. 'I know it's not right. You and me. But I want to try again. Please, Gabby. I love you.'

'What you want is your family life back. You like being a family man but you don't want me.' I thought of Dave and his thick, hard cock. It wasn't an effort for him to have sex with me. It was all sheer, delicious pleasure.

'I do love you. You're a part of me.'

The part that didn't function. *Oh God, I was getting nasty.* If this was Tony's idea of loving me, I didn't want it any more. 'I don't love you.' I stood.

'Gabby. No!'

I heard real pain in his voice.

He stood and tried to take my hand. 'Gabby, please. Stop being so angry.'

I jerked my hand back.

I saw desperation in his eyes. Fear. The dawning that I meant what I said.

'I have a right to be angry.' My jaw clenched so tight I thought I was about to crack my fillings. 'You have to take responsibility for your affair. Your affair has destroyed our family. I will not take you back because you don't think you have done anything wrong.'

'Gabby, shush!' Tony's gaze jerked worriedly around the café to see if anyone had heard me scream out the word 'affair'.

Several people were staring, but I didn't care. I watched as my husband's eyes filled with tears, the way they had when I nearly died.

This time I wasn't going back to him.

Did I feel victorious? No. Maybe I should have. After all, this was my moment of revenge. My time to tell him about the promotion Christine had offered me, the time to casually slip in that I was seeing someone who could satisfy me.

Instead, my throat tightened like I'd eaten something I was highly allergic to. There were tears threatening to prick at the back of my eyes. Damn my emotions. Somewhere inside me, I still had feelings for Tony even though I'd tried to cauterise them. My heart hammered. But what was the point? Even if I loved him for the rest of my days, my husband was a cheater. Some women were able to accept this in a marriage but I was too passionate a person, too dependent on the veracity of the situation and the truth was, Tony had no real remorse. I had to force myself to go on, to deliver the message I had come to give.

'Cami is missing you. I came here to discuss access, but we're both too emotional to work out anything long term yet. I want you to have Cami Saturday night because I need a break.'

'Gabby,' Tony choked out. 'Don't be crazy. Give our marriage a chance.'

'Don't ever call me crazy again.' There was a coldness in my voice that I'd never heard before.

After having post-natal depression, I was particularly sensitive to that word. I went through hell to have Cami: the miscarriages, the terrible birth, the emergency hysterectomy that followed, and even my time at The Clinic–the place where I had been labelled crazy.

I glared at Tony, full of accusation. It's a certainty that labels will stick, but does anyone ever ask what sent the person crazy in the first place?

7

When I had Cami nearly four years ago, I had no idea that I was going to lose my mind. Go *pazzo*! Crazy!

I now understand why mothers of newborns jump off cliffs leaving their child motherless for life. It's nothing to do with the baby. It's all to do with what is going on in your head. My head at that time was a dangerous place to be, but I was determined to cling on to my retreating soul because I knew that Cami needed me.

In a way, I'm glad I went through that momentary leap into insanity because the experience opened my eyes to a lot of things I had no idea about. It taught me what it was like to become a non-person, a ghost, in Tony's Italian family. My mother-in-law insisted that no one other than close family should know about this illness, leaving me feeling like a pariah.

But the illness taught me to search inside my deepest soul and find out who I was. I found strength there.

To me, bravery isn't taking on the baddies single-handed like they do in the movies. Bravery was clutching newborn Cami close against aching breasts and walking alone, severely sleep-deprived and anxious, into a mental hospital, nicely named, The Clinic.

The only time I had ever been in hospital, I'd had appendicitis. Tony had walked in with me holding my hand. After the operation, everyone in Tony's family visited bringing fruit or flowers.

This time things were completely different. In Italian culture, mental illness is shameful, something that must be suffered in complete silence. I knew something was wrong with me soon after Cami was born. Granted, her difficult birth hadn't helped. At first, I couldn't sleep and soon the days and nights became a blur.

Exhaustion is normal in motherhood, but when the suicidal thoughts started flitting through my mind like enticing whispers of escape, I knew something was wrong. Then the crying started. I couldn't stop the tears. I needed Tony, but he had a new job and had only taken a few days off work since I'd had Cami. Even the day I brought her home, he had only stayed home for an hour. In our culture, men are expected to work hard, especially when they are the sole provider of the money. Tony took his responsibility as the main provider seriously and increased his work hours. I barely saw him.

I was alone, alone, alone, and I hated it. Feared it.

Tony didn't get it, but he was worried about me and insisted he come with me to the six-week check-up. He asked my obstetrician, 'Can't she snap out of it? Gabby's usually so together.'

My doctor, with a concerned expression on his face, told him I couldn't. I had told him that too, but my words held no weight. Doctors are respected, so Tony listened to him. Somehow having a man tell him that I could have post-natal depression seemed to register more than me telling him that something was wrong.

My doctor thought I needed to see a psychiatrist. Wow, did this open a can of worms in Tony's Italian family.

It's better to have cancer than a mental illness.

My psychiatrist went through my family history to check if there was any mental illness there. As far as I knew, there wasn't. But how would I know? Mental illness is a banned subject in Italian culture.

'Tell me what you're thinking when you can't sleep?' the psychiatrist asked.

I didn't know how to answer that. I was exhausted. My head felt like someone was pressing their hands on my temples. 'I'm not thinking anything. I just want to get to sleep and I can't. I feel strange. I keep thinking about jumping off a cliff.'

'Why?'

'I don't know.' I never told him that Daniella's mother, Bisnonna, had cursed me, but I hadn't believed in the power of her curse then.

'Is your baby at risk?'

'No. I love Cami.'

'Did you want to have her?'

'God, yes. It took me years to get pregnant. I've had five miscarriages, a caesarean, and an emergency hysterectomy.'

The doctor thought the trauma of Cami's delivery had set off the post-natal depression.

He suggested I stay at The Clinic where they could monitor me while I took anti-depressant medication. I was desperate enough to agree. I was on my own all day with my baby. Alone. Alone. Alone. My mother-in-law couldn't understand why I wasn't coping.

My decision to go to The Clinic led to some interesting observations from Tony's family who were quick to criticise when they found out my psychiatrist's diagnosis. Pino stared at me in amazement and said, 'I can't believe that such a strong girl could get something like depression'.

Translation: Isn't that an illness for malingerers? Can't you use willpower to get rid of it?

Daniella brushed down her newly-blonded streaks and said, 'There's no mental illness in my family'.

I suspected that this wasn't the time to mention Daniella's mother, Bisnonna, who lived with her and had lost her marbles in the nineties. Old Bisnonna often walked around the streets in her nightgown wearing her wig back to front.

Tony did his usual thing. When I got emotional, he became distant. He pointed out a mother we knew who had eight children and said, 'Look at Maria. She's coping.'

Was Maria coping? Who would know? If she'd suffered any post-natal depression, she certainly wouldn't be foolish enough to admit it in our community.

The day I entered The Clinic, Tony drove me in but soon left for work once I was supposedly settled.

If I'd had cancer, I'm certain that someone else from the family would have stayed the day with me so I wouldn't have been so alone.

Perhaps I shouldn't have seen, *One Flew Over the Cuckoo's Nest*. It had coloured my judgement of what to expect in a clinic for the mentally ill. I had imagined disinfected linoleum floors, semi-comatose patients and burly security guards.

Nothing could have been further from the truth in the Mothers and Babies Unit. My room was nicely furnished with a single bed, shelving, carpeted floors, and a cot for Cami. There were no other mothers on my floor at that time, but I wasn't short of company. After my interview with the resident nurse, I walked into the lounge area and was surrounded by three svelte young women, Lani, Jennifer and Rachael, who fussed over Cami and begged to cuddle her.

'You're so lucky to have a baby,' enthused Jennifer. 'Oh I'd so love to have a baby. Is it wonderful being a mother?'

I'd barely slept for two weeks. When Cami slept, I was hysterical because no matter how long I lay in bed I couldn't sleep. I felt like I had drunk ten cups of black coffee and as I lay there night after night not sleeping, I wondered how I'd get through the day. And yet, when I saw the hope in Jennifer's face, I didn't want to kill her dream. Didn't want to see the expectation slide from her face by acknowledging that motherhood wasn't the experience I thought it would be-so I did what all mothers do to the uninitiated. I lied. 'It's great. She's a lovely baby.'

She was, but I was an alien. A heavy weight seemed to sit on my shoulders and I so lacked energy that even carrying Cami seemed difficult. My mind swirled with worries, all morbid and totally out of proportion to the problem. Physically, my stomach was still swollen from the hysterectomy. Squeezed into an elasticized skirt and large floppy shirt which hid my extended belly, I wondered if I would ever feel normal again or regain my figure; if I would ever be able to slip into tight jeans. Not that I'd had a model figure like these girls, but I still guiltily craved to have my old body back instead of this bloated, Jabba-The-Hutt post-pregnancy version.

Jennifer was squeezed into tight Mark Jacob jeans and a midriff top that showed off her flat belly to perfection. Like sylphs, the girls bent over Cami, petting her, admiring her little face. 'You're so lucky to have that terrific figure,' I said to Jennifer, my voice full of admiration. 'Look at you all. You're so slim. You look fantastic.'

The girls avoided my gaze. There was an uncomfortable silence. I wondered what I'd said wrong. These girls, especially

Jennifer, could grace the cover of Vogue. I felt frumpy just being in the same room with them.

A nurse came into the lounge area. 'Come on, girls. It's weigh-in time.'

The girls groaned.

I groaned, too. 'Weigh-in. Yuk. I swear I've put on ten kilos. I don't know what you girls are worrying about. Whatever you're doing, you should share it with me.'

'Vomiting,' Jennifer said.

'Taking laxatives,' Lani added.

'Binging and purging,' Rachael said. 'We're here because we've got eating disorders.'

'Oh! I mean...you look...I mean...you don't look like you're, er, thin, er, too thin.'

Rachael laughed. 'You should have seen me when I came into this place.' She shrugged. 'I've been here for months. You don't recover from this illness, you know.'

Lani rolled her eyes. 'I eat because I don't want to end up in the acute ward again. They keep the electric shock treatment patients there. It's horrible watching them afterwards.'

I looked into the eyes of these young women in front of me and realised they were far older than they seemed.

'We'd better take the lift,' Jennifer said, interrupting the uncomfortable silence.

'Can't risk losing any weight if we walk down the stairs,' Rachael added.

Alone with my foot in my mouth, I knew that while I appeared normal like those young women, I too lived in a world distorted by my worries and fears.

To distract myself I took the time to explore the ward, which consisted of ten bedrooms, a kitchen, laundry facilities, and a telephone in the hallway.

I stood in the hallway by the phone wondering what to do with myself. Uncertainty seized me. I was used to being surrounded by family. What was I doing here? I decided to ring Tony.

What was Tony's work phone number? I couldn't seem to remember the smallest thing. Though I had rung it many times, his number seemed to escape me, so I reached into the section under the phone where the telephone books were kept and pulled out a banana.

I stared at it in bewilderment. My arm started to ache from holding Cami. She snuffled against my breast reminding me that it was time to feed her. My heart contracted. I had decided to stop breastfeeding. Although this was more evidence of being a lousy mother, I'd decided to put Cami on the bottle because I didn't want to breastfeed her while I was on anti-depressants.

I looked down into my baby's face. Her mouth had made my T-shirt wet. The phone call to Tony would have to wait, but before I went to prepare her bottle, I bent and peered into the phone books shelf. There was an apple in there, too.

'Is everything okay?' I turned to see Lorena, the nurse who had checked me in.

'I just found a banana hidden where the telephone books should be.'

Lorena frowned. 'Those eating disorder girls, they hide their food everywhere. I swear I have to watch them eat every bite.'

'Is it all right if I eat it?' I was permanently hungry on my anti-depressants. I couldn't seem to walk past food. I no longer felt full no matter what I ate. It was as if my stomach never registered when I had eaten enough.

'Sure, but if you're hungry why don't you go down to the dining room for lunch? It's one floor down.'

She must have seen the indecision on my face. I had to feed Cami, but that wasn't the reason. I was scared to go by myself. Why? I have no idea. I just know that fear haunted my every move. Give me a baby and I had turned into a child myself. Confident, responsible me. Crazy!

'If you prefer, I can have something ordered up to your room.'

'I can't believe there's so much help here.'

For the first time, I didn't feel like I was being judged; that my motherhood skills weren't being assessed and gossiped about through Tony's family grapevine.

Six weeks later I left The Clinic, my sleep pattern and mood restored with the help of rest and medication. I decided that The Clinic wasn't so bad after all, but I guess I hadn't counted on the label 'crazy' following me home.

8

Dating was expensive.

I didn't like anything I had in my wardrobe and tonight was my big date. The things I'd taken so much trouble over choosing, my precious designer-on-sale bargains looked passé. My last season's Marc Jacobs pants were faded, my Alanna Hill skirt didn't seem right. I was suffering from a familiar complaint experienced by women who have a wardrobe full of clothes. I had nothing to wear.

Dave-the-underwear-thief had gone off with my only pair of sexy underpants.

I'd long ago stopped shopping at sexy lingerie shops. My underwear drawer was filled with sensible full cotton beige underpants designed to contain maximum amounts of stomach fat and not show a visible panty line. Mum bum undies.

Tony, of course, loved black lacy G-strings and suspenders, but he stopped buying that sort of thing for me after I'd had Cami and had become the Madonna.

I needed a makeover fast.

I needed something sexy to wear.

I needed my best friend, Lucy.

Lucy, who was a make-up artist, had cool taste. If anyone knew how to put a look together, it was her. And she owed me. I'd arranged a blind date for Lucy, who was divorced, with Tony's cousin on his mother's side. Lucy had been dating Riccardo for six months.

Two hours later, Lucy and I hit the department store on Pitt Street, looking for the perfect outfit. When I tried on Donna Karan, Lucy eyed me the way a wolf eyes a sheep, her gaze settling on my stomach. She handed two garments over to me. 'Try these, though you might be the next size up.'

'I'm a twelve in Donna Karan.'

'Try the next size up,' Lucy urged.

'No. This has to fit.'

'Does Bisnonna really have the Evil Eye?' Lucy asked me while I tried the dress on.

'Huh?' I stopped to reply. Well, I would have except I was stuck in the size twelve Donna Karan dress which wouldn't fit over my stomach.

'Try this.' Lucy helped pull the dress off over my head and handed me a black skirt and silver top.

'Just ignore anything Bisnonna says. She's going batty.'

Lucy's voice dropped though we were alone in the change room. 'But, Gabby, she pointed her finger right in my face and said: 'You no marry Riccardo.'

'What?'

Lucy thrust her hand in front of my nose. On her engagement finger was a two-carat diamond ring. 'Oh, my God! Lucy?'

My friend nodded with excitement. 'Riccardo's asked me to marry him. We're going to be cousins by marriage. Er...sort of. That's if you don't...um, divorce.'

I'd already filled Lucy in on my situation on the phone.

It seemed ironic that just as I was leaving the family, Lucy was joining it. Did she realise what she was getting herself into? What would someone descended from an officer of the First Fleet make of all the unspoken rules?

'So is it true, Gabby?'

'What?'

'Does Bisnonna really have the Evil Eye?'

I looked at my friend taking in her blonde hair and milky skin. 'You're an Anglo-Australian. You shouldn't believe in that stuff.'

'But, Gabby, Bisnonna didn't want Tony to marry you and look what happened. How many miscarriages did you have?'

'Five.'

'And you were so sick after having Cami.'

'Post-natal depression's common after a miscarriage.'

'But look what happened to your marriage. You complained that Tony couldn't make it with you.'

'We know he's not impotent. Ask Betty-Big-Boobs.' My voice was brittle.

'He is with you!'

'Lucy!'

'Sorry. I never said it was your fault.' Lucy blushed.

My hand snaked up to my *cornicello*, the horn-shaped coral amulet I wore around my neck.

'So do you believe in it?' Lucy insisted.

'I always wear this for protection,' I said, indicating my *cornicello*.

'So the Evil Eye is true.'

God, talk about persistent.

'Look, Lucy, I'm from Sicilian stock. I'm superstitious. It goes with the territory, but what I don't get is why you're worrying.'

'Bisnonna's ordered Riccardo not to marry me because I'm a divorcee. I mean, it's so dumb. Riccardo's divorced too, but she's not threatening to curse him. What am I going to do if she curses me?'

'Riccardo's proposed. You've got the ring. Don't worry about her.'

'But that's just it,' Lucy said. 'Riccardo wants to get her blessing or he won't go through with the wedding. He doesn't want me cursed like you.'

I dropped Cami off to Tony dressed in my day clothes on Saturday evening. Daniella opened the door and hugged me. Under the warmth, I saw sadness in her eyes. My poor mother-in-law had suffered enough with her rotten father, Pino's cheating, her crazy mother and now, me tossing Tony out.

Pino came to the door, kissed me and asked me to stay for dinner, which I politely declined, saying I needed a quiet night. Their combined warmth and continued acceptance made me want to cry, until I caught sight of Bisnonna who glared at me. She raised her index finger and little finger in the sign of the *cornuto* or cuckold. Did she know about Dave? How could she? I gave Cami a kiss goodbye, clutched my amulet and bolted home.

I was ready for my date on time.

I settled on a low cut, knock-him-out-with-my-boobies top and a slim-line black Marc Jacobs skirt, teamed with my Jimmy Choo shoes. Basically, I'd maxed out my credit card.

Lucy had taught me how to do my make-up. She'd insisted I do the 'Sultry Siren' look, which meant I had black eyeliner drawn up like blackbirds' wings at the side, metallic eye shadow and glazed-pink lips. Lucy liked the slutty-I-need-sex look and I didn't want to disappoint her.

Or me!

Lucy had given me heaps of free make-up, which was her way of apologising for dropping the little gem — the family thought I was cursed.

I'd always *thought* I was cursed, but no one in the family had ever told me. The admission jolted me.

When the doorbell rang I beat Bacci to the door even though I was wearing stilettos. Bacci sniffed and wagged her tail. Though she was harmless, she usually growled at strangers. I guess my dog had good taste in people.

I opened the door. 'Bisnonna! Daniella! What are you doing here? Is everything all right?' I looked beyond them but couldn't see Cami.

'It's Pino,' Daniella cried. 'He's in the ambulance. Heart attack. Have Bisnonna.' My mother-in-law pushed her mother towards me. 'I go hospital,' Daniella said, her English falling apart in her panic.

'But-but why can't Tony have her?'

Daniella threw up her hands. 'I call Tony. He no take mobile phone. *Ma che stupido.*'

She turned to go just as a black, shiny Porsche pulled into my driveway.

Dave stepped out dressed in a three-quarter, black leather jacket. His dark hair flowed around his shoulders. He looked like he'd just stepped off a runway in Milan.

Mamma mia! One look at him and I was full of red-hot lust.

'*Ciao*, Gabrrrriella,' Dave called to me.

Daniella stopped.

She looked from Dave to me. I saw her take in my sexy slut outfit. 'Gabriella. You go on date?' From her expression, I'm not sure what shocked her more, Pino having a heart attack or me going out with a man who was not her son.

Dave strode up the driveway. 'Is something the matter, Gabrrrriella?'

One roll of his 'r's' and my nipples tingled.

Bisnonna cackled. '*Bello.*' Handsome.

'Bisnonna, shush,' I said.

'I'm sorry,' I said to Dave. 'There's been an emergency. My husband–my ex-husband's father has just had a heart attack. Dave, this is my mother-in-law, Daniella, and her mother, Bisnonna. I need to look after Bisnonna while Daniella goes to the hospital.' *Oh, why me?*

'Gabriella. You have a man here?'

Yep. There went the sanctity of the marital home. Another unwritten rule broken. My husband had cheated on me, but I was supposed to be grieving, playing the shamed heartbroken wife; the one who couldn't keep her husband from straying. I should be wearing black rather than my *puttana* silver spangled top with my boobies half hanging out.

'Dave is a business client, Daniella,' I said.

I saw the disbelief in her eyes.

'I've had a promotion at work. I sell real estate now. Mr Angelo, er, Dave just bought an apartment from me.'

Daniella looked from Dave to me and back again.

'The penthouse in the Temple,' Dave confirmed.

'Go Daniella. I'll take care of Bisnonna. Pino needs you.'

Daniella took one look at my cleavage, crossed herself, and hurried back down the driveway.

'I'm sorry.' I turned to Dave. 'Daniella minds Cami for me. I have to help her in return.'

'Gabrrrriella. I understand family. We take Bisnonna to dinner.'

My mind whirled. Did I want to go on a date including Bisnonna? I'd rather have root canal treatment.

But Dave didn't wait for my response. Instead he turned to Bisnonna and invited her to dinner.

Her face flushed.

I watched in amazement as Dave offered her his arm. Would she take it or would she wave her bony finger in his face and utter a string of curses?

Bisnonna giggled like a girl. She linked her arm in Dave's and let him help her down the stairs.

My mouth dropped open.

'I'm coming,' I said to their backs. When I dragged Bacci inside, her tail slid between her legs in disappointment at not being included in the outing. I felt the same way. 'Wait for me...'

Dave turned and flashed me a smile. 'I hope you don't mind, Gabriella, if I put Bisnonna in the front of the Porsche.'

Mind? Why would I mind having Tony's old witch of a grandmother with us on my first and only date with Dave? God help me, but I knew after one night with her, he'd never be back.

'The Porsche doesn't have much room in the back for a little lady,' Dave explained.

It didn't have room for the fat rolls on my stomach either, I thought as I crammed myself into the back seat. My head hit the roof and I hunched my back. Personally I thought Bisnonna should stay in the back, or even better–the boot. That way it would be more difficult for her to take her clothes off should she feel so inclined.

* * *

Dave had booked Lucio's Ristorante in Leichhardt on Norton Street.

When the waitress took us to our cosy table against the wall, Bisnonna shuffled between us, grabbing the middle seat so that she separated Dave and me. She smiled at me, her dark eyes glinting with triumph.

I glared back.

I noticed her dentures had detached from her top gum. Would she choke on them? Maybe!

The Sommelier approached, handing Dave the wine list.

'You must have some pull to get us in here,' I said to Dave. 'The Herald said this restaurant has a five week waiting list.'

'It was easier than you think.' Dave glanced around him. I followed his gaze.

'Marble?' I could see dark lines like veins under the skin on the white floor.

'The best.' Dave nodded. 'After I selected the marble, I supervised the best tradesmen for this restaurant. Look at the workmanship. It's perfectly book-matched. You can't see where one piece finishes and the other starts.'

'You love your work, don't you?'

Dave leaned forward in his seat. He placed his hands on the table. 'Gabrrrriella, I am a passionate man. When I am involved, I make sure my client is one hundred percent satisfied, otherwise how can I be sure that the client will come back?'

I swear at that point shivers of appreciation tickled the bare skin of my arms. Dave reached over and took my hand. I could imagine Dave making love to me again. Even now his thumb was stroking the delicate skin on my wrist. He had a natural sensuality I longed to explore further.

'*Bello.*' Bisnonna pursed her lips to kiss him.

I snatched my arm away. 'Bisnonna!'

Dave laughed.

Bisnonna cackled.

I cringed.

I added a pap smear to root canal treatment as preferable options to this date.

Dave gave Bisnonna's hand a pat, motioned to the Sommelier and ordered wine.

While Dave was busy, I leaned close to Bisnonna. '*Basta*!' I said, ordering her to behave.

Bisnonna gave me the sign of the *cornuto.* In other words, the finger–Italian style.

I glared at her.

She glared back.

I broke eye contact first. I couldn't believe I was having a fight with a seventy-eight year old for Dave's attention. The trouble was–*she* was winning.

I scanned the menu the waitress handed me to look for something suitable for Bisnonna to eat. Milk-fed lamb? Soft but could choke her. A possibility. Salmon. Not enough tiny bones. Wouldn't do the job.

Dave picked up his menu and started explaining it for Bisnonna. She smiled and preened so that her wig sat askew and little tufts of grey hair escaped from under it.

'She's better to have minestrone and something soft afterwards,' I said to Dave, motioning to my teeth. 'And don't let her have too much to drink. Just a sip.'

'Let her have what she wants,' Dave said, ignoring me.

I frowned at him. He was an underwear thief *and* he didn't listen. Two strikes against him. Hmm. Lucky he was so good in bed.

'*Osso buco e polenta*,' Bisnonna squealed, sculling the half glass of wine that the waiter had just poured her.

I knew that the soft polenta would be fine for Bisnonna. But *osso buco*? If the meat was at all tough, she'd have trouble with her gums. 'Try the minestrone,' I said.

'*Osso buco*,' Bisnonna said.

What if she choked and vomited up her food on the table like I'd seen her do at Daniella's? I massaged my temples to relieve a stress headache.

'Guess that settles it,' Dave said with an easy grin. 'I can cut up the meat *fino*.' He motioned with his fingers to show he meant a small size. He patted her arm.

Bisnonna's cheeks went pink.

I watched how sweet Dave was with her. I had a sinking feeling that he was a nicer person than I was. When the meal arrived I watched as he diligently cut up Bisnonna's meat. She ate with such gusto that it occurred to me that perhaps she was sick of the minestrone and pureed meat that Daniella prepared for her.

At least with Bisnonna gobbling down her food, it gave me a chance to talk to Dave as I nibbled on my quail. 'You're so caring,' I said.

Dave shrugged. 'You're lucky to have family. I have no one here. I'm very lonely.'

Lucky. Me? Dave had no idea. 'Why don't you have a girlfriend?'

An expression I couldn't interpret flashed in Dave's eyes. Something hidden. In my state of lust I didn't think to delve behind the veil.

'I know what I want in a woman.'

He shot a look so intense I froze mid-swallow.

I took a gulp of my chardonnay and tried to control my choking so that the wine mixed with quail didn't make its way out of my nose.

Bisnonna chuckled.

'You see, Gabrrrriella, I'm looking for someone special.'

Oh no, here we go. 'Such as?' I asked, instantly on guard. Italian men with lists made me suspicious. Tony had wanted a virgin who was a saint like his mother. I'd thought that was an archaic cultural requirement not even plausible in Italy any more. I realised later it was because he was insecure about his lovemaking skills when he was younger and didn't want to be judged. Oh how I missed what we had learned together. All those wonderful moments of discovery.

'I need someone who understands Italy like I do,' Dave said. He waved his hand. 'I don't need to say, where else do you have such artists?'

Did Versace or Dolce and Gabbana count? Art bored me.

'I need someone who loves the culture, the food,' continued Dave, his gaze intent and intelligent.

I looked down at my stomach, which bulged over my form-fitting underwear. *No problem there.*

'Someone passionate,' Dave said, holding his fist to his heart. He leaned forward. 'Someone who wants a serious relationship.'

Gulp! *And here I was thinking he was just after good sex.*

'From the moment I saw you, I knew you would understand. You're like me. You're born here but you are Italian, too. You're sophisticated. Sexy. Young.'

Young? Didn't Dave realise how old I was?

'Why are you wrinkling your nose, Gabrrrriella? Do you not think you would suit me?'

'I'm...er...a bit older than you.' A bit? Was an eleven year gap just a bit? I guess it was, if I thought about the years as part of a long time line, like in history. I mean, eleven years are only a bit of time if I thought about when the dinosaurs were last on earth.

Dave raised his eyebrows. 'My last girlfriend was too young. When a woman reaches thirty, she is *bellissima*.' Dave took my hand and kissed my fingers.

'Er...thirty...'

'Hee, hee, hee,' Bisnonna chuckled.

I wanted to kick her under the table, but I was certain it was wrong to kick someone who wore white orthopaedic shoes. Anyway, how would I explain the bruises?

Dave's eyes softened. 'You're beautiful, Gabriella. When I first saw you, I knew you were made for me.

Gosh, this man was intense. Warning bells started to go off. I believe in lust at first sight, but from my experience love grew slowly.

'Barp!' Bisnonna burped loudly.

'Bisnonna!'

Talk about spoiling the moment. She sat back in her chair, hand on her stomach looking as satisfied and un-curse-like as I had ever seen her.

The waitress cleared away our plates.

I took a sip of my wine. My cheeks burned as I looked at Dave. I was feeling pretty damn good. Dave had given me more compliments in one night than Tony had in my last three years of marriage. I forgave Bisnonna her burp. It wasn't every day that I was told I looked like my favourite Italian actress. It certainly beat Tony's 'You need to lose some weight' or 'If I had a spare ten thousand dollars, you could get liposuction'. I knew these were the comments of a husband safely secure in his marriage, but I was so emotionally burned I needed the romance a new man could bring.

Dave was that man.

This date was working out better than I thought, especially considering I was being chaperoned like in the old country.

I smiled at Bisnonna. '*Buona?*' Good?

She smiled back.

Something was wrong. The *Jaws* soundtrack started playing in my head. Da-da-da-da-da...then I got it.

'*Bisnonna? Dove sono la tua dentiera?*' Where are your dentures?

I searched the table, the floor and right under the table where I saw that Bisnonna had taken off her orthopaedic shoes and was resting her crow-black stocking feet on Dave's ankles.

'Oh God, where are they?' I wailed. 'Daniella just paid a fortune for them. She'll kill me.'

'Bisnonna?' Dave asked, pointing to his teeth.

Bisnonna gave him a gummy smile.

'I don't remember her taking them out,' Dave said.

'They're not anywhere. Maybe she put them on her plate and the waitress took it away. I'll go look in the kitchen.' I stood. 'Keep an eye on her,' I ordered Dave. 'Don't let her go anywhere.'

Dave took Bisnonna's hand.

Bisnonna squeezed his hand and smiled at me, her dark eyes gleaming.

Witch! I frowned.

'Don't worry about her, she'll be fine,' Dave said.

Yeah, right! Wait until she starts stripping.

I raced as fast as my Jimmy Choos would carry me without slipping on the marble. I explained the situation to the waitress who showed me the garbage can where she had scraped off the plates. I stared at the garbage can. So did the waitress. It was full of sickening congealed food scraps, blobs of unrecognizable substances. It became clear that she had no intention of digging deep, nor did she offer me plastic gloves.

I squatted, the waistband of my skirt digging in tight, trying to ignore the slushy feeling on my fingers, the fat under my fingernails and the slime trails of food on my forearms.

Why did my life turn out like this? I was digging for dentures while a seventy-eight year old held my date's hand. How could I lift the curse? Dave thought I was thirty. Should I tell him the truth? With Dave I felt I had a shot at happiness and I so needed it.

I spied a yellow blob of polenta. Ha! The dentures. I hooked my finger around them and pulled them out. They looked like they were biting my finger; they looked like they were laughing at me.

I took them over to a stainless steel sink in the kitchen and cleaned the muck off.

I'd been unhappy for a long time with Tony.

Dave had been in my life such a short time, and yet, my life had changed for the better. I had my promotion, a better salary, and Dave. A man who was kind and generous, a man who made me happy. Not to mention drop dead sexy.

Even if this relationship lasted only a short time, I didn't want to let him go.

Even if it meant not telling him that I was eleven years older.

Even if it meant lying.

9

It was midnight.

Dave sat with his arm around me on my sofa regaling me with amusing anecdotes, interspersed with kisses. The warmth of his lips made my skin tingle. This wasn't how I thought my night would end. I thought we'd be having full-on passionate sex by now.

I resisted as Dave pressed me to him.

Across from us sat Bisnonna, her dentures clutched in one hand; her Evil Eyes observing us from under hooded eyelids.

Weren't oldies supposed to nod off?

My mobile phone buzzed and I leapt at it. 'Daniella. You're coming? Good. How long 'til you're here?'

'Daniella's on her way,' I said to Dave, slapping my mobile phone onto the coffee table.

'And her husband? How is he?'

'Pino? Er...I didn't ask.' What kind of a person was I? Dave asked about Pino and he didn't even know him. Yet I, so focused on seeing the back of Bisnonna, hadn't bothered. I massaged my temples.

'Daniella will tell us when she gets here,' I said.

Dave frowned.

'He can't be dead. Daniella would have told me that.'

'Don't worry.' Dave took my hand. 'I'm sure everything will be fine. Italian men are strong. We have fire in the belly.'

And somewhere else, I thought.

Dave's mouth curled into a sensuous smile. He leaned over and kissed me full on the lips.

'Smack!' Bisnonna pursed her lips.

'Bisnonna. *Basta*!' Enough!

Dave laughed, but I was having trouble seeing the funny side of being chaperoned at the age of thirty...er...I mean forty.

I was over minding Bisnonna, over Tony and his family. I had so little free time. Why couldn't I have one date with Dave without them interfering?

'Hee, hee,' Bisnonna cackled.

I wanted to smother her with her wig.

I craved to be alone with Dave. I could feel his body hard against mine; his hand warm and possessive. I was raw with emotional wounds and lust. A volcanic combination.

I wanted him.

I watched as Dave took a sip from his glass of red wine in a sinuous yet graceful movement. He was so perfect with his wide forehead, proud nose and sensual mouth that, sitting quietly there, he was almost a work of marble himself–a perfect sculpture.

With his long legs stretched out in front of him he seemed relaxed, but I wasn't fooled by his serpentine posture. He ran his forefinger up and down my wrist so that the tiny hairs rose on my arms and my nipples tingled. The look in Dave's eyes was intense.

He wanted me too.

When Daniella knocked at my front door, I sprang to my feet. 'Bisnonna. Daniella's here. *Alzati!*' I ordered her to stand. She stood and hobbled in front of me down the hall, clutching her dentures.

Dave stood too.

'Just stay there, Dave. No need to see Bisnonna off,' I said, trying not to sound as desperate as I felt.

I didn't want Daniella to see Dave.

God help me. Dave's presence at this hour would have repercussions that would rumble hrough our Italian-Australian community like an earth quake. I could imagine Daniella wailing: 'She had a man there. How long has she had a lover? My poor son. And she threw him out!'

I hurried down the hall, my fingers itching to prod Bisnonna so she would move faster. When I opened the door just enough to push Bisnonna through, I came face to face with Daniella. And Pino.

'Pino! I thought you were in hospital.'

'Indigestion. I tell him not to eat so much cotechino, but he no listen,' Daniella said.

'Indigestion?'

Pino shrugged. 'I'm an old man. We have disruption in the family.' He looked at me.

Translation: This is your fault.

'I worry,' he continued. 'It gives me pain. I think heart attack.'

Fart attack, more likely.

I noticed that Daniella tried to look past me down the corridor. There were questions in her eyes and, knowing Daniella, she intended to ask them.

I looked at my watch. I gave an exaggerated yawn. 'It's late. I'm tired. Time for bed. *Buona notte,*' I said. I closed the door in their faces, before they could ask me any questions.

I stood with my back against the door, eyes closed, my ears pricked like Bacci's, listening to them retreat. After twenty years of living the 'Italian way' with Tony's family, my metamorphosis to a more mainstream lifestyle was tough.

I knew I shouldn't have cared what my in-laws thought of me, but old habits die hard.

My life was intertwined with Tony's family and I had liked it that way. Pino invited us to dinner every Friday night and cooked fabulous meals. We celebrated every family birthday, every Christening, Easter and Christmas together, often with Tony's cousins–a small gathering, all forty of them.

We attended Mass every Sunday at the Sacred Heart Church. We shopped at the same food shops in Neutral Bay, went to the same doctors on Military Road. Pino went to Haberfield to buy our prosciutto and mortadella because it was better quality and cheaper than in the pricey lower North Shore delis. Pino even helped us get our housing loan from the bank.

Daniella had a key to our house, so she could bring over Tony's favourite pasta sauce while I was at work, and the extra home-cooked meal was always welcome.

My friend, Lucy, thought it astounding how much time we spent together. Pino and Daniella's intimate knowledge of our financial affairs horrified her. But as Pino and Daniella had generously helped us buy our house, it seemed normal to me that they would know what we owed on the mortgage.

'Spending money,' was Pino's favourite comment, uttered whenever Tony or I bought anything new instead of paying extra off the mortgage.

'Nosy parker,' was mine, but I never said it aloud. I knew that every cent had been important to Pino and his family who had nearly starved during the war.

I was used to living the 'Italian way'. In Brisbane, my father's brothers lived close. My father made sure my brothers bought in the same suburb by giving them their housing deposits. I was brought up to believe that family was everything, and even though the interference was annoying, I was used to it because I'd never known anything different.

Things had to change. I had to change and become tough like my boss, Christine. She once told me that to get over a man she took another. That sounded like good advice. It was time to become independent and Dave was part of that process.

I sauntered down the hall determined to pick up where I had left off- kissing Dave, not prodding Bisnonna out the door.

'Everything all right, Gabrrrriella?' Dave asked, still standing.

I nodded. 'Indigestion. Can you believe that?'

Dave tried to hide a smile. He failed. He pulled me close so that my body moulded into his and kissed me hungrily. That kiss touched something inside me. An aching loneliness.

I savoured the sensation of being held by him; of feeling his hot mouth possessive on mine. His body, lean and hard, was so well sculpted that as I ran my fingers up his back, I could feel every groove.

Dave broke the kiss.

He flicked open the button of my top exposing more cleavage.

'Gabrrrriella.'

His voice was almost a growl. In a few moments he had undone every button so that he could peel the slithery fabric from my shoulders. The top dropped to the floor with a soft plushing sound.

A reality check dimmed my passion. I thought about what my body would look like exposed against his in the bright light of my living room. Last time I'd had on my sexy underwear.

But lust fought back.

I grabbed his hand and pulled him along towards my

bedroom, needing the safety of my dimmer switch. Dave, however, had other ideas.

We didn't make the bedroom. He pressed me against the hallway wall, the cool plaster touching the bare skin of my back. In a moment my bra was off and his mouth was hot on my nipples.

I groaned and my eyes closed as he flicked his tongue over the tips of my breasts. His hands were all over me, undoing the zip of my skirt, hooking his thumbs over the waistband to include my underwear and pulling it down so that I stood in my hallway naked, except for my high heels.

The hall light glared above me. A spotlight on my nakedness.

Oh, good God, he could see every inch of me.

I looked down, but Dave wasn't studying my body. Oh no. Dave was kissing a pathway down my stomach, so that while his hair tickled my tummy, his hot lips sent shivers up and down my spine.

There was something so erotic about me being naked and Dave fully clothed.

I clutched his shoulders, the light fabric of his shirt a contrast to the strength of his shoulders. I closed my eyes. It couldn't get much better than this, I thought.

Then Dave got to his knees and buried his tongue in my cleft. I had never returned the favour in one of our sexual encounters but Dave didn't seem to mind. Maybe my braces put him off.

I could barely stand. My legs were trembling with each searing stroke of his tongue. My back was flat against the wall, my knees bent as he devoured me. I swear there seemed to be a psychic link from my brain to Dave's tongue because he knew exactly what he was doing: when to ease off, when to drive the tip of his tongue hard against my clitoris so that it swelled to a pearl.

Perhaps it was my moans of pleasure that guided him. Perhaps it was the way my fingernails dug into his shoulders. I don't know. I just know that when he ran both hands up the soft skin of my thighs and parted me with his thumbs, so that his mouth could possess me, I couldn't hold back.

I wanted everything he could give me. I imagined Dave naked, his cock hard and ready to fill me. I knew how good that felt. God knows, I was ready for it. As if sensing what I wanted, Dave pushed the length of his tongue into me. A moan started in the pit of my stomach as I clenched over it. I couldn't get enough of what he was doing to me. Already I was panting and writhing against his mouth, my butt muscles tightened as he returned to sucking my clitoris and slid his fingers deep inside me at the same time.

I swear I screamed as I came, but my voice was dislocated from my own ears. I was only aware of the intensity of what he was doing to me and that I could barely stand. The skin on my back was slick with sweat, my hands flat against the wall as I tried to remain upright.

I watched, unable to speak, unable to subdue my breath, as Dave stood and pulled off his belt. His eyes blazed with lust as he ripped at the waistband of his trousers.

I'd never wanted the cock of any man as much as I wanted Dave's.

Then I heard it. The key turn in my lock. My front door opened and Daniella's face appeared. 'I knock. You no hear. The dentures,' she started to say.

Daniella stopped. Her face turned white as she took in what was happening.

Dave covered me with his body, but I was barely aware of his protective move.

I had spied what Daniella was looking for. The dentures were lying at her feet, turned upwards like a disembodied curse of a smile.

Daniella's eyes dropped to where I was staring and she scooped down, picked them up, backed out and closed the door.

My orgasm, a small earthquake, was nothing compared to the seismic eruptions I knew awaited me.

10

'How could you bring a man into our family home, Gabriella?' Tony asked. 'My mother. My own mother saw you.'

Translation: You shocked a saint.

There was disbelief in Tony's eyes.

We sat on the bench in the park on the corner of Military Road and Cardinal Street, within the shadow of the Sacred Heart Church. I was a separated woman who had taken a lover. In Australian culture that was acceptable; in my culture, taking a lover so quickly made me a *puttana*, a whore.

Perhaps I was more Australian than Italian in that moment because I refused to let him make me feel like a *disgrazia*. A disgrace.

I raised my chin and stared my ex-husband down.

Tony broke eye contact. His shoulders were hunched with the pain of discovery.

He turned and looked at Cami who played happily on the swings just as she liked to do every Sunday after Mass. The Mass I had just avoided in order not to run into Tony's extended family. So much for not feeling like a *disgrazia*.

'I can't believe it.' He shook his head. 'The sheets haven't grown cold. You had a man in our house.'

'You're one to talk.'

'I never brought Betty into our home, into our bed.' Tony's voice shook.

People outside of my culture don't realise the Italian bed is sacred. I've never known an Italian adulterer to bring a woman into the family bed. I knew that while Tony had cheated on me, he would never have bonked in our bed. Did that make Tony's infidelity all right in his mind?

Bastard!

They say revenge is a dish best served cold. I liked mine hot.

I thought of Dave and of the delicious things he had done to me. A shiver raced up my spine. God help me, I hoped it wasn't over for Dave and me. After Daniella's rude interruption I'd been distressed and asked him to leave. Would he want to see me again?

'How could you, Gabriella?'

Tony's plaintive voice interrupted my thoughts. I should have said my love life wasn't Tony's business. I should have repeated that we were separated. But revenge made me cruel.

'We weren't *in* the bed.'

'Gabriella, please. My mother saw you.' Tony lowered his voice.

I cocked one eyebrow. 'Yes, she barged in uninvited and interrupted us in the hallway. Remind me to change the locks.'

Tony's jaw dropped. 'How long...you...him...how long...'

With infidelity, the moment of admission is sickening for the person on the receiving end. Painful. Brutal. I watched the emotions I had so recently experienced myself play across Tony's face.

It was all there: my betrayal; the dawning that he could so

easily be replaced when he'd thought he was irreplaceable. Worse. That I was capable of cruelty.

The rims of Tony's eyes reddened.

The revenge should have felt good. I waited for the blood to course through my arteries with victory. I wanted the rush of elation. And yet, I couldn't grasp the moment with triumphant hands. Instead, a dull thudding hit my heart. The back of my eyes turned hot. Did my own face mirror the hurt on Tony's? Tears pricked my eyes.

Damn! I wanted to be free of Tony's emotional grip on my heart. Every time I wanted to be nasty, the meanness stuck in my throat and choked me. I coughed, almost gagging on my cruelty. I wanted to crush any love I still had for this man. I wanted it cast out of my body.

Why was it so damn hard?

My eyes burned with tears.

I stood. 'Come, Cami. It's time to go home.' Cami looked up at us for a moment. She skipped over and sat on her father's knee, holding his hand and giving it fairy kisses.

'Coming home now, Dada?'

Tony shot me a look before turning back to her. 'Can I talk to Mumma a bit more?'

Cami nodded.

'Thanks, darling. You go play,' he said, setting her on the ground.

I watched as she ran to join the other children, out of earshot.

'I'm sorry for what I've done, Gabby,' he said, his voice sounding as if it had run across gravel. 'This isn't like you.'

'What do you mean?' I asked suspiciously. *What kind of an apology was that?*

'I've forced you into the arms of another man.'

'It isn't always about you.' Damn, Tony. Apologising then spoiling it by making it about himself. 'I'm enjoying Dave's company. He's very attentive. He seems to adore me and I've never had that before.'

My words were a slap to his face. He swallowed. His Adam's apple going up and down. 'Do you care about him?'

I stared into his soft brown eyes. 'It's new.' I didn't want to give details. This was my private life now and I had to set boundaries, which was difficult because I'd never done it before.

He looked at Cami for a moment before turning back to me. 'I've hurt you.'

Understatement of the year. Oh my inner bitch was dying to rear her head, but we had Cami and I was going to borrow from my civilised Aussie divorced girlfriends and try to still my tongue.

He stopped and swallowed. 'It wasn't because I wanted to.'

'Just say it. You don't find me attractive any more. I don't have a young girl's figure like I did when we met.' In a perverse sort of way, I wanted to hear him say the words, to cauterise any feelings I had left for him.

'You're beautiful. A gorgeous woman. So sexy. I don't want to lose you. I can't. You and Cami are my whole life.'

It was on my lips to say something trite, like *you should have thought of that before*, but the sheer, sharp pain he wore on his face stilled my tongue. 'I'm glad to hear you apologise. It helps a little, but it still doesn't change anything.'

'Gabby, you're my wife.'

'It takes a year to get a divorce, then I won't be.' I was harsh, but facts were the only medium I could deal in at the moment; emotion was just too hard. Underneath my raw pain I still loved this man, but I didn't want to. We had been through so much together and that had made a bond that wouldn't break.

'I love you.'

I stood. I couldn't bear the agony in his voice. 'I think you love me but your kind of love isn't enough. Without sex, we're friends and that isn't right for me. Not in a marriage.' I strode off before he could answer.

11

Late on Sunday morning, I sat at my kitchen table chopping the three onions needed for making Pino's delicious bolognese sauce, while Lucy, Italian-wife-in-training, assisted me. Both of us had avoided going to Mass. Riccardo had asked Lucy to come to Mass in a bid to get on the good side of Bisnonna. Lucy, because she wasn't Catholic, struggled with being a hypocrite. Me? I continued avoiding the family.

'So how is it going with Dave?,' Lucy asked, a twinkle in her eye.

'You heard about my date with Dave and Bisnonna, didn't you?' I pulled another board out of the cupboard, opened the refrigerator and took out the veal mince. 'Here. Spread that out on the board. Salt it. Pepper it.'

A guilty look flashed in Lucy's eyes for a moment before she picked up the salt and pepper. 'Did Daniella really catch you having sex?'

I sat back down and continued chopping. 'The secret of Pino's cooking is that he over-does everything and never worries about the calories. Lard, oil and butter are his main ingredients.'

'Did she, Gabby?'

'How did you hear?' I asked.

'Daniella told Riccardo's mother who told Riccardo who told me.'

'And the rest of the family at church.' I groaned. 'Yes, Daniella came in to get Bisnonna's dentures. She had a key.'

Lucy pulled a face. 'Riccardo saw you talking to Tony after Mass.'

'He wants me back, in spite of Dave.'

'And you? What do you want?' Lucy put the board on my kitchen table, opened the packet of mince and flattened it out.

'My boss, Christine, said to get over one man she took another. Do you think that works?' I stopped chopping.

My friend looked up at me with shrewd blue eyes. I knew that look. It meant something I didn't want to hear was coming. 'So what you're saying is that you plan to use Dave to get over Tony. You're not really that interested in Dave.'

'Quit making me sound like a bitch. I like Dave, but it's too early to say more than that. He's fun and kind. Part of me wants to see what it's like to be with another man. If I take Tony back, he'd move right in and nothing would change. He hasn't made love to me for three years. What kind of man doesn't have sex with his own wife?'

'Gabby, I don't understand it because I know Tony loves you. I can see it in the way he looks at you. Riccardo says Tony adores you.' She shook her head, looking at me with pity in her eyes. 'The trouble is, no one can ask him about it because we're not supposed to know.'

'I'm moving on, or at least I'm trying to.' I grit my jaw. I didn't want pity, so I changed the subject. 'Riccardo's nearly forty. Are you going to try for babies straight away?'

'I think so. I'd like to have two and I'm getting on.'

I winced thinking of Cami's hideous birth. How glad I was to have that behind me. I sliced through the onions making sure to cut them finely so they cooked evenly. Their aroma was delicious but they made my eyes burn.

The doorbell rang. I wasn't expecting anyone yet though Dave was coming for lunch with Riccardo and Bisnonna.

Lucy looked at her watch, shook her head and shrugged. 'It's too early. Riccardo is bringing Bisnonna at twelve thirty.'

'Penance for my bad behaviour last night.'

Lucy smiled.

At least my friend didn't judge me. She'd call me out if she saw me doing something she didn't agree with, but I didn't mind honesty. In fact, that was what I liked about her. I marched down the hall and opened the door to see a delivery man standing there with an enormous bunch of red roses. 'Could you sign here please?'

I walked back into the kitchen as I looked for a card.

'Who are they from?' Lucy asked.

'From Tony,' I answered, bemused. I put them on the kitchen table. I read the writing on the card aloud. 'I love you.' My heart twisted in pain. I moved back to the chopping board to get on with the pasta sauce or it wouldn't be ready for lunch.

'Wow. Tony's not giving up without a fight,' Lucy said. 'What if Dave wants to get serious, too?'

'What's wrong with having a simple affair with Dave?' I wailed. 'And why does Tony have to be so competitive?'

'Because the way I see it your husband is in love with you and Dave is all over you. It's not going to end well for someone,' Lucy said. 'All Tony talks about is how he can get you back.'

The knife came down too close to my fingers. My eyes stung. Tears started to roll down my cheeks.

'Don't look so happy about it,' she laughed.

I put the knife down, walked over to the sink to wash out my eyes.

'I'm happy to have a delicious affair. No complications. Dave's gorgeous.'

'So is an affair what Dave wants?'

I dried my eyes on a napkin. 'Add more salt. Turn the meat over and salt the other side too.'

'Does he, Gabby?'

I shrugged. 'How would I know? On our first date, Bisnonna was trying to jump his bones. We barely talked.'

I poured lots of olive oil into a heavy flat-based pan and cooked the onions until they were brownish, making sure they didn't burn. I breathed in the familiar smell with appreciation. An hour and a half later, the sauce was cooked and the doorbell rang. Riccardo, Bisnonna and Dave stood at the door. Dave carried a large bunch of red roses, and a box of chocolates which Bisnonna grabbed. I ushered them all in, looking uneasily at the roses, wondering if Dave and Tony had been to the same florist. Perhaps I should have hidden Tony's. Gosh, I hoped Dave didn't say anything when he saw them sitting on the kitchen table.

I should have been happy but an uneasy feeling came over me as everyone sat down. I served out the freshly cooked pasta and placed a green salad on the table. Illogical as the thought was, this scene seemed strange to me–Dave, in my home, surrounded by Tony's extended family and Lucy. Everyone was happy, so why didn't I feel that way?

It should have been Tony sitting there. Something twinged in my heart. I missed him, even though I didn't want to. The image of my husband hunched over with emotional pain played in my mind, like a bad re-run of a picture I didn't want to see again. I had hurt him so badly that now both of us were in pain.

I looked over at Dave.

Was this what I really wanted?

He smiled at me, his teeth flashing white in his handsome face, but I felt nothing in my heart. Dave as a lover. Certainly. I could manage that. With my feelings cauterised I could cope. But Dave as boyfriend...partner...a stepfather for Cami? She'd hate that. It would make her so miserable. I couldn't go any further with the thought. Luckily, Lucy was talking excitedly about her wedding plans and Riccardo was joining in with enthusiasm so no one noticed my silence.

'The wedding,' Bisnonna said, looking at Dave. 'You come.'

I hoped she didn't expect him to turn up as the groom.

'*Certo*,' said Dave. Of course. 'When?'

'Next week,' Bisnonna said.

'What?' I cried out.

Lucy let out a cry to echo mine. 'But Bisnonna, that's too early. I need to plan—'

'Next week,' Bisnonna repeated.

'Lucy. No!' Riccardo said. He knew better than to contradict Bisnonna. 'We'll do as Bisnonna says.'

'But...' Lucy began.

Riccardo made a chopping sound to cut off her protest.

Oh God, this was going to open a can of Italian worms. Dave and Tony at the same wedding. My temples throbbed. I tried not to think about it.

'Your family is so respectful,' Dave said to me. 'In Italy, no one seems to care what the older people think any more.'

'Everyone cares what Bisnonna thinks,' I said.

'You're a good person, Gabriella. So nice to Bisnonna. Thank you for inviting me to meet everyone. This is a lovely family.'

Dave had no idea.

I waved away Riccardo, Lucy, and an unwilling-to-leave Bisnonna clutching my chocolates , at three that afternoon.

'Mission accomplished,' I said to Dave. I reached up and

kissed him. 'You made Lucy and Riccardo very happy today. And thanks for putting up with Bisnonna.'

'Bisnonna's not so bad,' he said. 'She reminds me of my grandmother back home.'

I bet his grandmother wouldn't have tried to tongue kiss him goodbye!

I snapped the security lock across the door and leaned against it with a sigh of relief. I wasn't taking any chances that my few hours alone with Dave would be disturbed.

I was guilty. In fact, I was riddled with a Catholic guilt so strong that I was convinced I would burn in the fires of hell, but that didn't stop me pulling Dave into the bedroom the moment everyone left. When Dave was near me, I wanted to be naked with him. I was obsessed.

I didn't think it was love. What I felt for Dave was nothing like what I had felt for Tony. This was a chaotic passion that I seemed to have no control over, right from the moment I laid eyes on him.

I had two hours before I had to go over and pick up Cami and I wanted to make the most of them.

Dave slipped his loafers off. 'Ouch!'

'What?'

'There's something on your bedroom floor.' He picked up his foot and pulled out something embedded in his skin.

I put my hand to my mouth. 'Don't worry, it's not glass. It's just some rock salt. Cami spilled the packet this morning,' I lied.

There was no way I was going to own up to sprinkling rock salt around my bed in a bid to ward off a witch–otherwise known as Bisnonna. Nor was I going to own up to the piece of amethyst or the three pieces of rock salt which currently resided in my pocket.

'Ouch!' Dave stepped on another piece. He hobbled over to the bed. 'You need to sweep your floors, Gabriella.'

I ignored the ripple of irritation that raced up my spine. How dare Dave tell me how to keep my house?

I pushed the thought aside. My brain was on fire. All I could think of was sex. I pulled off my dress in one clean sweep. Underneath it I wore the latest in La Perla, a lacy mauve bra and matching G-string, which complemented my olive skin. Dave lay on the bed and whistled.

Hope Dave didn't think he was going to steal these undies.

I looked down. For the first time in years, my stomach was flat. Unlike everyone else, I'd gone easy on the carbs over lunch. The lust diet was in full force.

'I hope you're not going to stay fully clothed. You seem to be making it a habit,' I said.

Dave gave me a slow, sexy smile and pulled off his simple black T-shirt, then slid out of his jeans and boxers. He already had his made-to-order erection. In his hands he fingered a condom.

Watching him disrobe was enough to make me wet.

I never lost my sense of amazement when I saw his body. The way his stomach muscles contracted into a sixpack made my mouth water. He spread out on my bed, his dark-coloured hair on my pillow, watching me. The man was a poster boy for all things sexy and Italian.

'Lose the bra, Gabrrrriella. 'Slowly. Let me see you take it off.'

I did as he asked, remembering a time when I didn't want him to see me naked. My insecure thoughts no longer cut through my confidence. I had Dave to thank for that.

He motioned forme to come over to him.

I lay down beside him so that my back curved into his stomach. One of his hands roved over my body, lingering on my breasts, down past my rib cage, over my hip and in between my legs.

I opened my legs to let him explore. What I liked about Dave as a lover was that I rarely had to speak. He was intuitive.

He pushed my G-string to the side and slid his fingers up and down.

I reached backwards to guide his erection inside of me. Keeping my hand on his hip as a guide I rocked back onto him, squeezing and keeping his cock deep inside of me. 'Don't move,' I ordered. I used him, enjoying every moment of it by creating my own rhythm, pushing his cock further and further inside of me until I hit the spot I wanted.

Dave's breathing grew heavy. I was certain he wanted to thrust by the way his hand gripped my hips.

He groaned. 'Gabrrriella.'

'Don't move,' I said. Two could play this game.

I rocked back onto him, building my rhythm, dominating Dave with my sexual needs. His cock was hot inside of me.

I came with an intensity that had me crying out loud. I lay panting as Dave watched me, with what I swear was a slightly desperate look on his face. 'You did well to stay so still.'

'I nearly came so many times,' he said as he began to climb on top of me.

'Wait a minute.' I pushed him off. Dave looked at me, puzzled.

The naughty side of me wanted to test him. I couldn't help myself. 'I haven't finished yet.' Although G-spot orgasms were always great, there was nothing like multiple clitoral orgasms for me. I reached into my side drawer and pulled out a girl's best friend–my vibrator.

Dave's eyes widened.

I switched it on, pleasuring myself as he watched me. I don't know if I shocked him. I would never have done this to Tony because he would have taken it as a personal insult that he couldn't satisfy me. But Dave was younger than me and this gave me the courage to take the initiative–to be the boss. He didn't speak, which was unusual for Dave. His hand went down to his bulging erection as he watched me.

'No. Don't touch yourself,' I ordered. 'This is payback.'

'*Che?*' What?

He probably thought it was because he'd ordered me about sexually before, but it wasn't. 'Never tell a woman she needs to sweep her floors.' *Especially an Australian woman of Italian heritage.* Anyway, I was saving that fantastic erection for my pleasure.

Dave shook his head but, I'll give him credit, he smiled until the smile dropped from his face and was replaced by red-hot lust.

I rubbed the vibrator over myself, moistening it with my juices until it slid freely over my clitoris. I was already swollen and hot and it didn't take long to come. The ferocity of my orgasm amazed me. White heat rolled over me until I was screaming in pleasure.

Head spinning, my arms flopped to my sides when I could take it no longer.

Dave drove himself into me as if he couldn't contain himself. Arching his back and growling, he came in what seemed like minutes.

'You are *the* most sexy woman, Gabrrrriella,' Dave said. 'You have–how do you say it–no inhibitions.'

'Mmm,' I said.

'I have never seen a woman use a vibrator,' Dave said.

'Mmm,' I said.

'That was fantastic for me,' Dave added.

'Mmm.' I was never a great conversationalist after sex. In that way, Tony and I were compatible. He had liked to fall straight to sleep after we had sex, back before Cami was born.

Unlike Tony, Dave was sensuous. He stroked my nipples and kissed my cheeks in a loving way. I loved him touching me. I closed my eyes and floated on a sea of sensuality, unaware of time. Unfortunately, Dave also liked to talk.

'How can Lucy and Riccardo plan a wedding so fast?' he said, changing the subject from sex. 'In Italy we take months to put a wedding together.' Dave proceeded to tell me about his sister's wedding, not sparing a detail.

I dozed.

Dave nudged me.

'Mmm?'

'What do you think, Gabrrrriella?'

I had no idea what he had just asked me or how long I'd slept.

'What?' I blinked sleepily at him.

'I was telling you about my mother.' Dave stroked my face, which was lovely.

I could feel my eyes closing again. I hadn't had such a relaxing afternoon in a long time. I could even sleep through Dave's continuous talking.

'The way she cheated on my father with his best friend before I was born.'

'What?' How had I missed that? My eyes snapped open. 'Why would she do that?'

'I was telling you,' Dave said with a frustrated frown. 'I like the way you're so forgiving. You're good to your ex's family.'

I thought of the pain Tony's family were in at the moment over our split. 'We've had our differences, but they've been good to me, especially Daniella.'

'My mother is never grateful for what my father does for her. Nothing makes her happy when she has so much to be happy for.'

I frowned at Dave. Why was he telling me this? Did I want to know about the pain in his family? If this were Tony speaking to me I'd want to know, but Dave, despite our intimacy, was still a stranger in so many ways.

'My mother makes problems for everyone.'

I looked into Dave's eyes. The gorgeous green colour had turned into a sea of trouble. 'You see, Gabriella. I am not my father's son.' Dave pulled me close so that I could hear his heart beating hard in his chest. 'That is why I came out here. My mother told me I looked like her lover. It hurt her to be reminded of his face.'

'What? Your mother sent you out here?' What a bitch! Poor Dave. And yet, his problems didn't touch my heart, the way they would have had it been Tony.

Instead, I wondered what the time was. I sat. I wanted to look at my watch to see if I had time to have a shower before I picked up Cami.

'Thank you for asking me over today,' Dave said, still lying back on my pillows, watching me as I rose and pulled on my robe. 'On Sundays, back home, I usually spend time with my friends,' he said.

'You're lonely,' I said, turning to face him. 'Why didn't you bring someone with you?' Dave didn't seem to enjoy his own space the way Tony did–or peace and quiet either.

Dave sighed. 'Who would I bring? My father manages the business back home. My mother doesn't want to see me. My sisters are married with their own families.'

'I don't know how a gorgeous guy like you is single.'

'I wasn't,' Dave said. 'I...I...' His voice caught. 'I wanted to marry my girlfriend...to have a family...*con molti bambini*...with many babies. She was too young for that, I think.'

There was something in his eyes, an expression that told me not to go there.

So I did.

'What happened? Why did you break up?'

'She left me. Told me I suffocated her.'

I should have taken that as a warning, but my brain was pleasantly floating in an orgasmic soup.

'That's so mean,' I said, my voice full of sympathy.

Dave got up and hugged me close. 'I love you, Gabriella.'

I froze. I knew he wanted me to answer him. I knew he wanted me to hold him close and say I loved him too, but my tongue wouldn't move.

'I...I...' I stuttered.

I felt his arms tense around me. I saw the hurt in his eyes. I cared about Dave, but was that love? The feelings I had weren't the same as I felt for Tony, but Dave was a different person and this passion was different.

Somehow, when Dave walked into my life, good things started happening to me: my promotion' a pay rise' my reference for my real estate course. I felt happy and light with Dave around me because he didn't come with baggage that affected me. Besides, I was having the best sex of my life.

For the first time since the birth of Cami, I was a strong, sexually-confident woman again. I was happier than I had been in a long time and being with Dave was part of that. I didn't want him to walk out of my life.

I pushed myself away from him and looked at my watch. 'I have to go to Daniella and Pino's to pick up Cami.' *When all else fails–take off.*

'I want to meet your daughter. I miss the little ones in Italy. We go together.'

A wave of irritation washed over me. Didn't Dave get it? We'd made love and it was fantastic, but now I had to get on with things alone. I didn't need to be with him every second of my day. Besides, Cami would freak out if she saw another man cuddling me. I couldn't do that to her. Sure, one day, I'd have to introduce her to someone if he was special enough, but was Dave that man?

'Look, Dave, it's...it's too early.'

I saw annoyance flicker across his face.

'Everything is too early for you, Gabriella. You introduce me to your friends, but you won't introduce me to your daughter.'

He cupped my face, his eyes unhappy.

'Tell me you love me, Gabriella.'

I couldn't. Not now. Not yet. I wasn't certain that it wouldn't be another lie. Already, my age was a lie.

'Look Dave, I can't have you in every part of my life. You have to go slowly. My child is just coping with the fact that her father and I aren't together.'

Dave's hands dropped from my face. 'What you want from me, Gabriella? Am I nothing more than sex for you?'

Dave's English became more stilted when he was upset. He looked around, located his clothes and started pulling them on.

My throat tightened as I watched him dress. I didn't want to fight, not after the day had worked out so well. Dave was important to me. He'd made Lucy so happy. I was confident and relaxed around him, but I couldn't live with myself if I told him any more lies. It wasn't fair to him.

'I really like you. You know that.'

'No, I don't, Gabriella.' 'This.' Dave pointed dramatically at the bed. 'This is what we have. But you, Gabriella.' He pointed at my heart. 'You give me nothing. You are not Italian in your heart. You feel nothing when I talk to you.'

Dave snatched his keys off my bedside table, walked out and slammed the door behind him. I heard his Porsche roar off into the distance.

I wondered whether I would ever see him again.

12

I woke in the night, my heart splitting in two. Dave was wrong about me. I felt plenty. The trouble was - it was for the wrong man. I missed Tony.

Dave was too possessive. Alone here in Sydney he was like an immigrant starting out, making friends and contacts, but I couldn't be everything to him. I didn't want to be.

I reached out beside me in the bed. My hands grasped at cold empty sheets. Of course they were. Tony and I had split up and I was not going back to him.

Tears poured down my cheeks in the dead of night and I couldn't seem to stop them. I was in mourning for what I had lost, and yet, I refused to forgive Tony because nothing would change if I did. He would only be unfaithful time after time like Pino. I accepted that, but why did my lack of forgiveness hurt me so much?

Why did it leave me feeling like an empty shell?

When I arrived at work the next morning my desk was covered with papers and something else. More red roses. A bunch so luxurious that it hid the chair behind it. Guiltily, I wondered which man had sent them. Dave hadn't said anything about Tony's roses but that didn't mean he hadn't noticed them.

I heard the familiar click of high heels behind me. 'Someone is popular,' said my boss, Christine.

I'd told her that Tony and I were no more, but I hadn't told her about Dave. To give her credit, Christine had decorum. She didn't rush over to open the envelope to see who had sent them the way Tony's nosy cousin Gia would have. I knew they wouldn't be from Tony. Big gestures weren't his style.

Something this spontaneous could only come from Dave. Not that I deserved them, seeing as I hadn't returned even one of his ten calls to my mobile phone. I walked over and opened the envelope. It said: *I know I ask too much too soon. Forgive me. Meet me. The Temple 12 o'clock. You have my heart, Dave.*

Did I want his heart?

I couldn't answer that question. I just knew that my own was beating way too fast at Dave's summons. I glanced at my schedule. I had an appointment at twelve. No matter. I'd cancel it.

I had to meet Dave face to face so I could explain to him why it wasn't a good idea for him to come to the wedding. Would he finish with me?

Would today be my last time with him?

Damn it. It really pissed me off that I might have to end this affair with Dave because of Tony. I really liked Dave and I'd gone without sex for so long. Tony didn't have the right to control my emotions. I had to toughen up. How did some women disconnect the emotional from the physical? I had no idea. I certainly wasn't good at it.

. . .

Around one, Dave walked me back to the office. The sky was bright blue, a lovely day for Sydney. The noise of the traffic didn't bother me nor did battling the lunch-time crowd on Martin Place. I swear I was floating on a cheerful cloud.

Dave must have seen the smile on my face when we reached the office door because he reached over and squeezed my hand.

'Don't kiss me goodbye,' I warned. 'My boss doesn't know about you.'

'Why not?' He frowned. 'Why haven't you told her about us?'

'Because you're a client. I don't want to lose my job. I only just got my promotion.'

'I understand.' He gave my hand another quick squeeze then let it go. 'I'm out of town tomorrow, so I'll see you Thursday looking *bellissima* at the church.' Dave kissed his fingers in an Italian gesture.

Oh no! I'd forgotten to talk about the wedding or, more specifically, Dave not going to the wedding.

I watched him proudly pull out the invitation from the inside pocket of his leather jacket. 'This came by courier this morning. I called straight away to let Lucy's mamma know I was coming.'

'Er...you did?'

No doubt Dave noticed the smile slide from my face. 'What's the matter, Gabriella?'

'You see Dave...um...this is Tony's family too. I just don't think it's such a good idea if you come...because...it's disrespectful to Tony. I meant to talk to you before...but...um, I forgot.'

'Tony is not your man any more. I am your boyfriend. I want him to see that.' Dave thumped his chest. For such an exquisite-looking guy he really could come over quite primitive at times. 'I will not insult Lucy and Riccardo by refusing their kind invitation.'

Nor the old witch I suppose.

'I will not disappoint Bisnonna.'

Thought so.

'Fine. Come then. But if Bisnonna is having a bad day, don't be surprised if she thinks she's marrying you. If she tries to kiss you, I'm not saving you.'

We stood glaring at each other. Damn it, he was needy.

My office door opened. Christine stood there. 'Good afternoon, Mr Angelo,' Christine said, shaking Dave's hand. 'Everything all right, Gabriella?'

God, she must have seen us arguing. 'Um...yes. Everything is fine, thanks, Christine.'

'So tell me, Mr Angelo, you're still happy with the apartment?' I knew from Christine's expression she was worrying about losing the commission.

'Of course. It is *magnifico*. I love it.' Dave waved his hands in a grand gesture.

'And you are happy with Gabriella showing you around again?'

Thanks for checking up on me, Christine.

'But of course. Gabriella is very good.'

Phew! I needed Dave's praise just then to save my arse. It wouldn't look good if Christine thought I argued with clients.

Dave beamed his approval of me to Christine and patted me on the shoulder.

My heart sank. I couldn't believe it. Why hadn't I seen it earlier? Caught in Dave's front teeth sat one of my black pubic hairs.

13

'I feel like calling off the wedding,' Lucy said. I looked over at her. We were each lying on a massage bed having a hot rock massage at Lucy's health spa in Double Bay. It was Lucy's idea to relax her pre-wedding nerves. Despite the therapist's best efforts, I could see it wasn't working for her.

'You can't do that. Think how it would hurt Riccardo,' I said, shifting slightly as my therapist placed two deliciously hot rocks on my shoulder blades. God knows, if anyone needed to relax her over-sexercised body, it was me.

Lucy scratched a hive on her neck. 'But Gabby, this is meant to be my dream wedding and you wouldn't believe the stuff Riccardo's mother is insisting we have.'

Oh yes I would. I thought of Daniella's sister, Rita, a big woman with over-blonded hair and enormous breasts. While Daniella was stylish, Rita was loud. She would insist on the best wedding for her only child, Riccardo. Unfortunately, Rita's idea of what constituted the best was different from Lucy's.

My therapist put two hot rocks on the base of my spine. 'Mmm, that is good.' I was suffering from multiple-orgasm butt ache.

'Are you listening, Gabby?' Lucy said, raising herself on her elbows so that the rocks balancing on her shoulders slipped off and dropped to the floor. Her normally pale complexion was flushed. I noticed her therapist give her a look, but she didn't say anything. Wise woman. The air was filled with friction despite the New Age flute music and muted lights.

'I'm hearing you, Lucy. Look, if you give in to Riccardo's mother you are setting the pattern for your whole marriage,' I warned her. 'Rita will want a traditional Italian wedding, but it's your wedding, not hers.'

'I've already given in to getting married in a Catholic church.'

'I know that wasn't easy for you,' I said soothingly.

'I've said no to the doves. I've said no to the throwing of grain.'

'How did she take it?' Somehow I couldn't imagine anyone saying no to Rita. She'd puff up like a toad.

Lucy grimaced. 'Not well. Look Gabby, I know this is your culture and I respect that Riccardo comes from an Italian background, but Rita is really upsetting me. She's insisting my mother carry a bag so people can put money in it.'

'*La borsa*,' I said, thinking of the silk bag that I had carried at my own wedding. Family and friends had paid to dance with me. It was an enjoyable custom. The money had come in handy too.

'Can you imagine my mother doing that?' Lucy shifted. Her hot rock flew off her back and hit the floor with a crack. 'She'd die before she asked people for money.'

I thought of Lucy's mother, a face-lifted Darling Point matriarch. 'Er, no. I can't see that. You could carry the bag yourself. All the men will have to pay to dance with you. It's a lot of fun.'

'Gabriella! I don't expect people to pay me to dance at my wedding!' Crack! The last remaining rock flew off Lucy's back. The therapist shook her head. Lucy gave me such a look-you would have thought I'd asked her to enter into prostitution. *Mamma mia.*

'So have you settled on the food?' I asked, changing the subject.

'I planned such a beautiful menu but Riccardo won't let me have nouvelle cuisine.'

Which meant Rita wouldn't.

'We're having antipasto, pasta, salads, meat, fish, lobster, fruit, some fried dough thing, pastries, cakes, endless coffee. I can't remember all the rest. How can people eat so much?'

My traitorous stomach let out an enormous growl. I'd barely eaten anything all day in my efforts to be slim.

'Gabriella!'

'Sorry. I can't help it. Your menu sounds delicious.' Lucy wouldn't understand that nouvelle cuisine wouldn't cut it with Italian-Australian guests. They'd think she and Riccardo had financial problems if they didn't provide a feast. Pity she wouldn't carry *la borsa*. Riccardo's worried relatives would have it stuffed full of cash by the end of the evening even if she only served three courses.

Lucy scratched at a hive on her cheek. 'My mother thinks it is outrageous to serve so much. Wasteful.'

Lucy's mother was stick thin. Lucky bitch. 'Sweetie, tomorrow is going to be the best day of your life. You have a beautiful dress and Riccardo loves you. I know the food seems extravagant, but putting on a feast is going to make Riccardo so proud of you.'

For the first time I saw my friend's shoulders relax. The therapist shot me a glance of approval. 'Do you really think so, Gabby?'

'The best day. It's going to be a fantastic wedding, I promise you. Think how happy you're going to be as Riccardo's wife.

Think about your dream of having children.' I watched as my best friend's face softened into a smile.

The therapist started massaging Lucy and gradually her face lost the strained look. Inside, I prayed that everything would go smoothly and that Lucy would be happy. We couldn't afford to have a neurotic bride on her wedding day. Goodness knows Lucy had a neurotic matron-of-honour, though I was trying hard to hide it.

I wasn't looking forward to the wedding. Tony and Dave coming face to face.

I so wasn't ready for that.

14

My heart was in my mouth as Lucy and I arrived at the steps of the Sacred Heart Church for her wedding. The park in front of the church was a cool green backdrop in the evening light, but the vista did nothing to calm my nerves.

You see, I was the scarlet woman. At Lucy's insistence I bought the crimson dress that, according to Lucy, went so nicely with my complexion; perhaps it was not such a subtle choice given my situation. I wish I'd realised it earlier. Lucy looked the antithesis of me with her blonde bob and her virgin-white wedding gown, the silk falling over her subtle curves, while mine were encased like Gabrielle from *Desperate Housewives*.

'You look beautiful.' I gave Lucy a kiss on both cheeks before I assisted her with pulling her wedding veil over her face.

This was Lucy's second marriage and I wanted to tell her that this time it would be forever, but my tongue seemed to be stuck to the roof of my mouth. I could feel tears forming in the corners of my eyes. How could I tell her that when I no longer believed in love lasting forever? I didn't want to enter this church where I knew Tony would be standing at the altar waiting, dressed in a similar black suit to the one he'd worn at his own wedding, while I wore this sexy crimson number.

All the memories I had tried to suppress came flooding back as we climbed the stairs. I had walked these steps so many times: when Tony and I started dating, for my own wedding, for Cami's baptism and for the regular services that I attended with Tony and his extended family.

The church was beautiful, a graceful and solemn edifice, a place of faith, love and peace, but for the first time I couldn't gain any comfort. It wasn't that I had given up my faith-I just felt I no longer belonged. My heart pattered in my chest like a frightened rabbit's. I could feel sweat dripping between my breasts even in the cool night air. Were my cheeks as crimson as my dress?

'It's all right, Gabby,' Lucy said. She gave my hand a squeeze.

'Lucy? Do I look nervous?'

'It's the way your eyes are darting from side to side, that's worrying me,' she said.

Yeah, looking for the escape exit.

'I'm sorry. I'm trying to be calm for you.'

'Don't worry.' She squeezed my hand. 'I'm calm. I want to marry Riccardo. It was planning the wedding so quickly that was stressing me out, but now it's done. The best thing is I haven't let Rita get her way with everything.'

'Good.' I massaged my face muscles to calm myself, but I was so tense I felt like I'd been to the taxidermist.

'Remember what you told me last night,' Lucy said, giving my hand a last squeeze. 'It's going to be a fantastic wedding.'

'Of course.' I'd become adept at lying since my marriage broke up, but I didn't say that.

The organist started playing 'Trumpet Tune'. The wonderful music that I'd had at my own wedding filled the church. Its sonorous sound lifted my spirits. These people weren't here to look at me; they were here to see the bride.

While they were gazing at Lucy, I'd be searching out where Dave was sitting. Hopefully he'd be in the back of the church, as far away from Tony as possible.

I walked down the aisle in front of Lucy, trying to keep my pace slow so that Lucy could remember and enjoy every moment. I saw many faces I recognised-shop owners, local people and well-wishers sitting at the back of the church. No Dave. Where was he?

Towards the centre of the church sat lots of children, cousins and second cousins, aunts and uncles and relatives who had some tenuous link to Tony's family. They were all staring at me. Their heads turned to observe me, their dark eyes, and a few blue ones, followed me up the aisle. No one was smiling. It felt like blackbirds were pecking at my back, drawing blood bright enough to match my gown. Shouldn't they be looking at the beautiful bride rather than the scarlet woman? Was I having a Catholic-guilt paranoid moment?

I spotted Cami sitting on Gia's knee.

'Mamma!' She wiggled up and down.

I blew my precious daughter a kiss.

I continued up the aisle. Still no Dave.

In my nervousness, my mouth had gone dry as I neared the front. I tried not to cough. I stared across the front pew as I approached, where I knew Tony's family would be sitting.

I nearly tripped as one of my shoes caught on the hem of my dress. I steadied myself. Dave was sitting up the front next to Bisnonna with Daniella and Pino. A wave of displeasure shot through me.

He was trussed up in black tie that didn't suit his free and easy dress style. He mouthed hello and I barely had time to respond because I noticed something else. Bisnonna was wearing something glittery on her head. I stopped, even though I should have kept walking. I looked closer until I strained my forty-year-old eyes. Bisnonna was wearing a small tiara on her head. It wasn't much bigger than a dramatic hair clip, but I was sure it was the tiara that had kept my veil in place for my wedding with Tony, the tiara I kept safely stored at Daniella's home.

What was Daniella thinking of, letting her do that?

I looked at Daniella. She rolled her eyes and shrugged her shoulders. Couldn't she control her crazy mother any more?

Bisnonna grinned at me. Her face looked crinkly and old as she held Dave's hand. Was she a parody of what I was — an older woman with a younger man? Would I look like an old lady if I married Dave, wearing bits of glitter in the hope of making myself look younger?

Aware of Lucy coming up behind me, I forced myself to keep walking. A new thought hit me like a blow: everyone here would know how old I was. There weren't many secrets in Italian families. Which one of them would tell Dave the truth about the difference in our ages?

When would Dave learn that I was a liar?

I stumbled forward to take my place to the side of the altar. I didn't want to, but I couldn't stop myself. I sought out Tony — the man who was still my husband. He stared at me and I saw something in his eyes that I hadn't expected to see–a look of love.

Oh God, why couldn't I stop loving this man? Loving him was useless because I wasn't going back, even if Dave and I didn't last.

If anything I needed time on my own.

Tony gave me a gentle smile.

In spite of myself, my heart leapt to see him before I had time to force it into the lack-of-response mode I demanded from it. Tony looked gorgeous in black tie. He always did. A thought hit me. I knew why I was having this neurotic Catholic-guilt moment.

In my mind, I was still married.

Why, oh why couldn't I emotionally disconnect from Tony?

I saw Riccardo beam as he caught sight of Lucy. Why wouldn't he? This was meant to be the happiest moment of his life. But for me–all I could feel was that I was a failure. I had failed to keep my marriage together and all these people were here to witness that.

I had failed to forgive my husband for his infidelity. I couldn't. I couldn't be a good wife, follow in Daniella's footsteps and look the other way. I still cared for Tony, that was the problem; even being with Dave couldn't erase that as much as I wanted it to.

I listened, my head bowed, as the priest officiated over the wedding Mass. Unlike others I knew, I loved going to church. At least I did before my marriage broke up. Every vow Lucy and Riccardo made was a barb to my heart. 'To love and honour,' Lucy repeated after the priest.

I loved Tony but I didn't honour him any more and he didn't honour me. If he had, he wouldn't have had an affair with Betty. Did he really love me? If he did, how could he be unfaithful? Why wouldn't he have sex with me? The unanswered questions swirled round and round in my mind.

I thought of Dave sitting behind me. I had been brought up by my Italian mother to believe that if I were to have sex with a man, I should love him. It was like that in the old days for my mother who had adored my father. But my mother had passed away and I was grown up. I enjoyed my lustful relationship with Dave, yet Tony still had an emotional hold over me. It was distressing, caring about two men at the same time.

Was that how Tony felt when he had the affair with Betty?

Distressed? Perhaps she really meant nothing to him. Had he learned from Pino to have affairs without feelings?

I thought about Pino sitting there with his hands clasped over his big stomach. No matter how much he had hurt Daniella with his affairs, he didn't seem uncomfortable with it. Perhaps men got used to the feeling of betrayal until their infidelity no longer stirred their conscience. I didn't know. I just knew that I couldn't cope with how I was feeling. I wished this wedding service hadn't churned up my emotions like a writhing sea washing up refuse from the deep.

I watched as Lucy and Riccardo exchanged rings. I had never seen Riccardo so animated in his expression. Despite the haste of this wedding, I was sure that Lucy would think it was worth it. She'd probably even thank the tiara-stealing Bisnonna.

Riccardo lifted Lucy's veil and kissed her. There were sighs of appreciation amongst the guests. Over Riccardo's bent head, I caught sight of Tony. He wasn't admiring the bride and groom. He was staring straight at me. He smiled again. 'I love you,' he mouthed.

Oh God, that was a stab to the heart. Why did he have to say that to me? In this church, under the eyes of God? It affected me more than if he had been angry with me for having Dave there. How could he keep being so nice to me? I didn't deserve it. I really didn't agree with Christine. Taking on another man didn't help my situation. It didn't stop my feelings for Tony though I had hoped it would. It just made it more complicated.

The priest announced Riccardo and Lucy as man and wife. When they turned to walk back down the aisle, I swear that the attention of everyone was focused on me and Tony walking down the red carpet, rather than the bride and groom.

Tony's shoulders rubbed against mine as we walked. 'You look beautiful, Gabriella.'

I couldn't move away from him short of walking into the

wooden pews. 'How could you tell me you love me under the eyes of God? You have to stop this. You need to let me go.'

'I do. You're so sexy, Gabriella. Vibrant.'

'Why would you care? You never did anything about it,' I snapped. *The tension was getting to me.*

So the scarlet woman appealed to him, did it? What was it? The competition?

It felt intense to have my husband so close to me as if we were partners again. Extreme emotions boiled around inside of me. How did poor Dave feel watching us together? I searched him out and caught his smile. Then Tony did something that made me catch my breath. It happened just as I met Dave's gaze.

Tony took my hand.

Bisnonna cackled.

Pino and Daniella nodded their approval.

The smile dropped from Dave's face.

Tony walked me down the aisle, holding my hand so tightly that I couldn't pull it away. He made sure that the whole community could see that he had a stake in me, leaving Dave to follow us down the aisle with Bisnonna clutching his hand.

Once out of the church I yanked my hand away from Tony's. 'Did you have to do that?'

Tony just smiled. His eyes gleamed. I had never seen him so competitive.

I turned my back on him and stalked over to Lucy and Riccardo. 'Congratulations,' I said, through gritted teeth.

'It was a lovely service, wasn't it?' Lucy gushed, apparently having forgotten that she hadn't wanted to get married in a Catholic church. 'It's so beautiful here at night,' she added, looking over the park which was lit up with lights. In the background the traffic hummed on Military Road.

Suddenly a flash of white hit the night sky. Doves! Hundreds of them took to the air in mad confusion.

'Shit!' Lucy said under her breath.

One confused dove flew close to Lucy's face. She screeched, warding it away and leaped back into Riccardo's arms.

'Aren't they beautiful, Lucy?' Riccardo kissed her. 'My mother organised that as a surprise for us. Kind isn't she?'

From the expression on her face, Lucy looked like one of the doves had pooped in her mouth instead of on her veil. I grabbed the clean handkerchief out of Riccardo's pocket and quickly wiped the offending poop off Lucy's veil before it dripped onto her face.

'Was that what I thought it was?' Lucy asked.

'Don't ask.' I saw Rita bustling towards us, her arms outstretched. 'Riccardo. *Mio figlio.* My son.'

'Dove poop is lucky,' Riccardo said, happily. 'Our marriage is blessed. *Mamma, vieni qui.*' Mum, come here. He embraced and kissed his mother.

'It's good luck,' I said, to reassure Lucy.

'What *is* bad luck in your culture?' Lucy asked, examining her veil.

'*La mia nuora.* Daughter-in-law.' Rita squashed Lucy to her big bosom.

I looked at Lucy's rotund mother-in-law. There was the bad luck, in my opinion.

Rita kissed Lucy, took hold of her veil and ripped it.

'What are you doing?' Lucy gasped.

'*Buona fortuna*,' Rita said.

'More good luck,' I translated.

Lucy's blue eyes nearly popped out of her head. 'But I like my veil,' she said, examining the tear.

'Er, maybe I should have warned you about that custom.' I was aware of people jostling me out of the way to get to the bride and groom. 'Prepare yourself. Extra good luck is coming your way. All the men will want to kiss you.'

Lucy was about to reply but she was engulfed by a sea of well-wishers determined to kiss the bride. I stepped backwards to let them at her.

Sydney has wonderful places for wedding receptions, but the Venetian Trattoria on Darling Harbour wasn't one of them. The Venetian did have stellar views of the Harbour and a large enough room, decorated with red-checkered tablecloths, to fit the two hundred people who could be gathered together at the last minute. Due to the short notice, only Lucy's parents had managed to come, the rest of the guests were Riccardo's.

I knew that Lucy had wanted tasteful white tablecloths and flower decorations made up of her favourite gardenias, not grapevines on red-checkered tablecloths. She must have changed her mind and not told me.

I stood with Lucy, Riccardo and Tony, receiving guests. It wasn't usual for Italian-Australians to do a receiving line, but this was what Lucy wanted.

'This is nice,' Dave said as he entered the restaurant on the arm of Bisnonna. 'Very Italian. Very like home.' He shook Riccardo's hand, gave Lucy a peck on the cheek. Dave pulled me to him and kissed me full on the lips in front of Tony.

'This is Tony,' I said, trying to readjust my gown and wondering if my lipstick was smeared all over my face. My stomach rolled with nerves.

Tony shook Dave's hand politely but his were glinting.

Dave nodded, his look a rapier.

If someone had lit a match at that moment, I swear the air would have caught fire.

Bisnonna cackled, but at least she didn't make things worse by doing the sign of the *cornuto,* the cuckold. Slowly, she cast her

Evil Eye from me to Tony to Dave. I trembled. Tony swallowed nervously. Dave had no idea what was going on.

'*Bello*,' she said, patting Dave.

'*Stupido*,' she said to Tony, slapping him on the cheek with a crack.

Bisnonna tottered off with Dave leaving the bridal party open-mouthed in her wake.

'Tony, did she just call you stupid?' Lucy asked.

'Don't go there,' I hissed.

'Best not to,' Riccardo said.

'Hmph!' Tony said, rubbing his cheek.

I liked Bisnonna at that moment, even with her tiara. *My* tiara. I never thought she'd see things my way.

'Your string quartet in the corner there is lovely,' I said to Lucy, changing the subject. 'Very tasteful.' Rita had wanted to organise a dance band to play tarantellas, the dance of the ancient spider, but Lucy had nixed that. Pity. I liked to dance, but it was Lucy's wedding.

'It seems to be the only thing I ordered,' Lucy said, casting a sideways glance at her mother-in-law 'Where are my nice white tablecloths? My flowers?'

'Rita?' I said quietly.

Lucy's eyes narrowed. 'Rita!'

Waiters gathered in the trattoria to welcome guests with trays of liqueur for the women and hard stuff for the men.

'What happened to the trays of champagne?' Lucy asked, bewildered as she stood beside me. 'They're supposed to serve champagne.'

'It's just an aperitif. Italians expect it, Lucy,' Riccardo said. 'Don't worry, the champagne will come out next. Mamma organised things this way.'

Rita bustled over to Riccardo. 'You like?' she nodded at the drinks. 'I pay extra. I organise drinks, tables, music.'

'Very nice, Mamma,' Riccardo said, kissing his mother.

'Did she just say music?' Lucy asked.

Just then an Italian-looking man, wearing a black jerkin and three-quarter pants with a red sash around the waist, walked in carrying a mandolin. If I didn't know better I'd have said he was there to play the Tarantella. Now I adore the old ways, and I was glad that the Tarantella had made a revival in Australia, but I could see from the look on Lucy's face that she didn't share my enthusiasm.

I grabbed a couple of shots of liquor off a nearby tray. 'Here drink this,' I said to Lucy as I gulped one down. Lucy followed my lead.

'How could you let your mother take over our wedding?' Lucy hissed at Riccardo, while Rita was chatting animatedly to guests. She hit Riccardo on the pocket. 'Ow! What have you got in there?' she asked, rubbing her hand.

'Iron,' Riccardo said, tapping his pocket.

'*Tocco ferro,*' Tony said, putting his hand to his crotch.

'Pity it didn't work for you,' I said to him under my breath.

Tony didn't bite at my nasty remark but his eyes deepened until the pain showed through.

I bit my lip. 'I'm sorry,' I muttered under my breath. There was no need to be cruel.

Tony cast me a hurt look and I wondered what it was that he wasn't telling me. Why couldn't this man make love to me?

'What was that, Gabby? What did you say?' Lucy asked, interrupting my thoughts. 'I missed that comment.'

'More good luck,' I said 'The iron is supposed to ward off the Evil Eye. Plus give luck in the bedroom, but that's just my take on it.' I didn't look at Tony.

Riccardo grabbed his crotch and leered at Lucy, but somehow I got the feeling she wasn't sharing in his enthusiasm.

'What do I use to ward off your mother?' Lucy asked him, instead.

'Lucy, calm down. It's an Italian wedding. Apart from your parents, only my family has shown up. It's going to be fun,' Riccardo said.

Riccardo had a point, but I didn't think it was tactful of him to rub it in.

Lucy and Riccardo were soon swamped by well-wishers again, which stopped them arguing. Daniella kissed Riccardo and Lucy. Pino caught her up by the waist and gave her two smacking big kisses. His joy was infectious and in spite of herself, Lucy gave a squeal of laughter.

I accepted my mother-in-law's kiss of greeting, but avoided her eyes. I liked Daniella and I didn't want to see her pain. It must have cost her to see Tony and me together at the altar. She was a good person and I knew our marriage break-up would be hurting her. She was dark under her eyes as if she hadn't been sleeping. In my culture, when a couple breaks up, the whole extended family feels their pain.

I grabbed another shot of liquor as Daniella walked past. I was willing to resort to Dutch courage to calm my nerves. Thanks to Bisnonna, Tony hadn't dared misbehave so far. But would he be able to contain himself over the insult of my lover attending the wedding in front of his family and friends? I'd thought he could when I'd discussed it with Lucy earlier in the week, but after I saw the way he'd looked at Dave I wasn't so sure.

I noticed that Tony was resorting to liquor shots like I was. '*Cento anni di questi giorni* one hundred years of happy days,' Tony called, leading the toast by lifting his glass.

I swallowed another glass of liquor on an empty stomach. Lucy attempted to swallow hers, but she had no opportunity as all the men were lining up to kiss her again.

In spite of Rita's takeover of her wedding, Lucy flushed with pleasure as everyone fought to kiss her pretty fair cheeks. Although a lot of the guests were from Northern Italian stock, with fair to ruddy complexions, Lucy still stood out with her slender figure, pale skin and naturally blonde hair. Riccardo's bride was a hit.

'Remember how happy we were?' Tony stood beside me, watching Lucy and Riccardo. 'We were just like that at our wedding. In love.'

Goosebumps rose over my body. 'Don't ill-wish them with your envy,' I warned him.

'I'm not, Gabriella. You know I'm not.'

I looked at my husband and saw his eyes were moist.

'I just want us back together again. I want to go back to a time when you didn't hate me,' Tony said.

'Infidelity is like a knife,' I said quietly. 'You only know how bad it is when you feel the blade.'

'I know I hurt you,' Tony said, glancing over at Dave. 'I drove you into his arms.'

What could I say to him? I didn't want to hurt him any more because I still loved him and I always would, but I had to stand up for myself. My husband needed to learn that infidelity wasn't okay. Something to be treated lightly. For the first time, I saw the real dawning of pain in his eyes, as if it had finally occurred to him that there was no hope for us.

He hadn't seemed to understand that there would be a consequence for his actions. 'I'm not a saint like your mother. I won't let you treat me like Pino treats Daniella. I deserve better.'

Tony shook his head. 'That was never my intention. I love —
'

I waved my hand at him to stop him talking. 'We can't keep discussing this. You need to move on.' I could feel the familiar acid pain burning in my stomach. Although I wasn't hungry, I needed to eat something or I'd end up with an ulcer. I walked off to sit at the bridal table, leaving him standing there, his mouth open with a reply that I didn't care to hear.

I sat on Lucy's left hand side while Tony sat on Riccardo's right. That placed me as far from Tony as I could possibly be. In front of the bridal table, Lucy had placed Dave, Bisnonna, Lucy's parents and Pino and Daniella together.

I could see Bisnonna beaming as Dave looked after her by filling her glass and holding her hand. The hardship she wore on her face dropped away and she almost looked pretty. Daniella gazed on in wonder as she observed how patient Dave was with Bisnonna. For this alone, I knew she would respect Dave. Everyone was scared of Bisnonna, but was anyone but Daniella kind to her?

I shook my head, amazed at Dave's ability to remain charming under Tony's glowering eye. Daniella even laughed at something he said. I glanced at Tony to see how he was coping. My breath stopped. Tony slugged back a glass of red, his hand hardening around the rim of the wineglass until I wondered if the glass would snap.

Oh hell.

The food was beginning to arrive, the first of many courses, but I couldn't swallow a thing. Would Tony leap over the bridal table and take Dave by the throat? The look in his eyes was growing more dangerous by the minute. How hard was it for him to watch even his mother enjoying Dave's company?

A terrible sadness tore at my heart. I wasn't good at revenge. I didn't like what this was doing to Tony.

Antipasto arrived — a course consisting of olives, Stracchino cheese, salami, mortadella and prosciutto, followed by spaghetti bolognese; then *spezzatino* (a veal and vegetable dish), *pollo arrosto* and *insalata* (roast chicken with salad) and *pesce* (fish stuffed with breadcrumbs, garlic and parsley).

'This food is amazing. I'm so glad I decided not to go nouvelle cuisine,' Lucy said, conveniently forgetting it had been Rita's idea. 'I think I'm going to burst out of this dress.'

'Eat less,' I said, glancing over at Tony. My heart was in my throat.

'What is it, Gabby, you're not touching your food?' Lucy asked.

'Tell Riccardo to stop Tony drinking.'

She glanced across at Tony and looked back to me with her eyes wide.

'Oh my God. I've never seen him look murderous. Think I should get Riccardo to move the knives?'

I put my hands to my face. 'Why did we give in to Bisnonna and let Dave come?'

The musician with the mandolin accompanied by two female tambourine players appeared on the stage. 'The Tarantella is starting,' I said to Lucy.

'But I hired a disco. What happened to that?' Lucy's face held a bewildered expression as if she couldn't comprehend all the changes, let alone the possibility that Tony was about to commit murder. 'They have my waltz music. Riccardo and I have been practicing for weeks.'

'Ask Tony to dance,' I ordered her. 'He won't refuse you. If he's dancing with the bride, he can't kill Dave.'

I watched Tony slug back another glass of red. He flicked off his cufflinks and rolled up his sleeves. He eyed Dave, flexing his accountant hands into fists. Had I driven my non-violent husband to craziness? 'Lucy, please!'

'But I don't know how to dance the Tarantella,' she wailed.

'It's easy. It's a circle dance. You start clockwise until the beat changes. Look at the tambourine players. They're showing how it's done.'

The dance was said to cure madness and eradicate the body

of poison from a spider bite. Given the poisonous energy I could feel emanating from Tony, it would come in very handy right now. I nudged Lucy. 'Pretend you've been bitten by a spider. If you don't dance you'll die of its poison.'

'And that's a wedding dance? Whatever happened to the bridal waltz?' Lucy said, getting to her feet. 'And what about Riccardo? I should be dancing with him.'

'Hurry, Lucy,' I begged.

'All right.'

I watched as she bent and whispered something in Riccardo's ear. He looked over at Tony and nodded, his eyes concerned. 'Get up, Gabriella,' he said to me. 'Dance with your husband.'

I didn't want to dance with my husband. I didn't want to give the impression that we were together, but I realised that Riccardo was right. I couldn't expect the bride to lead the Tarantella with the best man. That would seem absurd.

Riccardo took Lucy's hand and led her onto the dance floor. He knelt at her feet and everyone clapped. Lucy looked around her as if she didn't know what to do, but I saw her catch sight of one of the tambourine players swinging her skirt and twirling. Lucy copied the tambourine player by holding her skirt wide and twirling around Riccardo.

The crowd cheered with appreciation. I saw family members rise to their feet. Riccardo put his hand on his heart and blew his bride a kiss. He looked proud, virile and delighted with his wife.

My hand went to my mouth. My eyes were hot with emotion. Behind me I was aware of Tony's presence. I was acutely conscious of how bitter my own heart was towards him, as I watched this show of love.

Riccardo leapt to his feet and did some elaborate spins around Lucy. She laughed with delight. Cheers went up from the crowd again.

Riccardo extended his arm to me and Tony, encouraging us to

join him. It was unlucky to dance the Tarantella alone. The more that other people joined in the better. I took a sharp breath. I looked at Dave. Would he understand that I had to dance with my husband although he was no longer the man in my life? I'd much rather dance with Dave if Bisnonna would let me.

Dave stood and held out his hand. I saw Bisnonna clutch at his arm and short of prising off her arm, Dave was caught.

Tony gave me a slap on the rump to get me moving and I jumped. I swear I felt I had been bitten by a tarantula–the Italian wolf spider- myself.

Everyone laughed.

I rounded on him, but before I had time to speak, Tony took me by the hand and pulled me to the dance floor. I saw Dave scowl as he watched me with my husband. How long would he be able to remain polite?

'If you get down on your knees and do that beating heart thing like Riccardo, I'll walk off. I won't have you pretend that you love me,' I hissed out of the side of my mouth.

Tony took a sharp breath. Perhaps my words penetrated his alcohol-filled brain because instead of making the dance an elaborate show of courtship like Riccardo had done with his bride, he linked arms with Lucy and we started moving into the circle dance.

Bisnonna pulled Dave to his feet and rushed as fast as her orthopaedic shoes would carry her towards us.

Dave glared at Tony.

Tony's arm tightened possessively on mine so that I couldn't pull away without making an enormous fuss, which I wouldn't do. Not for anything would I spoil Lucy's wedding.

Dave's eye's narrowed until he looked like a fiery god of a man, with his dark hair flowing around him and his muscles bunched under his tuxedo.

I held out my free arm to Dave. I had Tony on one side and Dave on the other. Soon the dance floor was packed with everyone linking arms so they could join in.

We moved clockwise to the sound of the mandolin. I could feel Tony's arm muscles tensing as he pulled me along with him, which made it difficult to keep linked with Dave, who was moving at a slower pace because of Bisnonna. Dave's arm muscles tensed too, so that he pulled me away from Tony. But Tony was determined not to share me and pulled me hard in the direction of the dance so I was forced to break the link with Dave altogether.

I looked over to see him still arm in arm with Bisnonna. Dave scowled fiercely. His eyes narrowed at Tony and I swear if Bisnonna hadn't kept a claw-like grip on him, he would have been at Tony's throat. I never thought I'd be grateful to Bisnonna.

The beat changed signalling the change in direction. I dropped Tony's arm and ran to join Dave so I could link back up with him. Tony moved swiftly to rejoin with me, pulling me close to him, until I thought I would break in two.

The mandolin player kept up a crazy pace. The tambourine players whirled around as if poisoned by the spider's bite.

Everyone was laughing, trying to keep up with the beat. Eventually the mandolin played so fast that no one could keep up. Everyone fell apart laughing and spinning off in different directions.

I should have been laughing too, swept up with the happiness in the room, but I wasn't. I was only aware of the discord of the dance and how well it imitated my life. I thought my heart would break as the two men fought over me.

I snatched my arm away from Tony's, anxious to get away from him. I was too passionate a person to be able to pretend.

We'd had a pretend marriage for the last three years and that wasn't good enough for me.

My heart was filled with hatred for Tony at that moment.

I hated the way he tried to act that we were together so that he wouldn't lose face in front of his extended family. I couldn't stand his determination to win, to have me with him because that was the right thing to do in the eyes of his family. It was as if I belonged to him by right. His possession.

To hell with him!

Why couldn't he do the thing I wanted? Why couldn't he explain why he had been unfaithful and ask my forgiveness instead of just assuming I would overlook it, like Daniella had done so often with Pino? Why couldn't he prove to me that he loved me so much that he would never stray again? Why couldn't he make love to me? That was what I wanted. I stumbled back to the bridal table.

What I hated most was that he still had the power to affect me. Did I still love him? I didn't know. I just wanted not to care about him. I wanted my heart to be free from his grip.

'Are you all right, Gabriella?' Dave asked, coming towards me.

'Did you have to pull at me like that?' I rubbed at my arms.

'I won't let him have you.' Dave hugged me to him.

I looked over at the dance floor where Tony stood glowering. 'I don't want to be with Tony and his family. I don't want to be here.'

'Gabrrrriella. I know this is hard for you.'

I lay my head against his chest glad for the feel of his arms around me. Glad to breathe in his warm smell.

'I had to be here because of Lucy, but I didn't want to come.'

'I know. I came to look after you,' Dave said reassuringly. He rubbed my back like a little child and I didn't care who saw us. I needed every ounce of comfort he could give. But my dose of comfort was short-lived as Bisnonna soon found us together.

'*Vai via,*' go away, she said to me, clawing at Dave's arms.

I dropped my arms from Dave and she grinned at me triumphantly. 'Hee, hee, hee.'

She held his hand.

Dave gave me a weary smile.

Poor Dave. 'You're a good person,' I said. 'Kind.'

Dave shrugged in an Italian way. 'Be strong, Gabrrrriella. We'll leave as soon as it is polite. This is just a few hours. We will have many hours together in the future.'

His lovely words should have given me strength, but I wasn't convinced that we could have a future together, not with the lie of my age standing between us. Not with Dave wanting kids.

Cami ran over and I picked her up. I kissed her on her plump little cheek and she put her arms around me. 'Dave, this is my daughter, Cami. Cami, this is Mamma's special friend.'

Dave smiled into my eyes.

'*Ciao*, Cami,' Dave said to her, giving her the informal Italian greeting. 'I've been waiting to meet you. Your Mamma tells me many good things about you.'

'Say hello, Cami,' I prompted my daughter.

'*Ciao,*' Cami said, but she was somewhat distracted.

She looked from Bisnonna to Dave. 'Bisnonna, why you holding that man's hand?'

'*Fidanzato,*' Bisnonna said, informing Cami that Dave was her fiancé.

Just then, Salvatore, Gia's boyfriend, weaved his way towards us. Whatever he'd been drinking, he'd clearly had too much.

Despite my fondness for Tony's cousin Gia, who was terrific with Cami, I didn't understand what she saw in her Sicilian-Australian boyfriend of two years. I'm from Sicilian stock and I love my brothers who are charming men, but I disliked Salvatore. He had a wiry build with long limbs, which reminded me of a spider. This coupled with a sarcastic sense of humour, which he'd tried on me, had led to me ordering him out of my house some months before.

Salvatore stared at me boldly; the way a man does when he wants to ask questions of a sexual nature. 'So, Gabriella, we're trying to work out what is going on here. Who are you with?' His lips curled in a smile as if he thought himself clever at being brazen enough to ask me what others had not. He looked from Dave to me.

'There is a young person here,' I said, my voice full of warning, 'who doesn't know the full circumstance of our relationship.'

Dave stepped forward. 'I am Dave Angelo,' he said, introducing himself, holding out his hand to be shaken.

'Gia says this is your new boyfriend,' Salvatore slurred, rudely ignoring Dave's outstretched hand.

My arms tightened around Cami.

I saw Dave's outstretched hand take the shape of a fist.

God, don't tell me he was about to start a fight at Riccardo and Lucy's wedding. That was the last thing I needed. I put my hand on his arm to steady him. I could handle this.

'No,' Cami said, patting my chest. 'This not my Mamma's boyfriend. That man Bisnonna's boyfriend.'

'*Fidanzato,*' Bisnonna corrected Cami. Bisnonna smiled, her shoulders thrown back proudly. Her face glowed with glee.

Although there was no love lost between us, Bisnonna was seventy-eight. What harm did it do for her to be happy even in her warped, bizarre way?

Salvatore slapped his thigh. 'That's a good one. Your fiancé.' He laughed at Bisnonna.

Bisnonna's face crumpled.

'Go away, Salvatore,' I said.

'You get around, don't you,' he said to me. 'Do you share him?' he asked crudely, looking from me to Bisnonna.

'And you,' Salvatore said to Dave. 'What are you doing with that old woman?'

Hell! *Was he talking about me or Bisnonna?* This was getting way out of hand. I looked around for Gia. I wanted her to get rid of her stupid boyfriend before Dave drew attention to us by thumping him.

I knew there would be trouble at this wedding but I wasn't expecting it from this quarter. The family never treated Bisnonna with disrespect. They knew better, but Salvatore wasn't family and I hoped he never would be.

'Apologise,' Dave growled.

'Leave it,' I said to Dave. 'He's had too much to drink.'

'Apologise or I take you outside and make you.' Dave stepped up to Salvatore, clearly itching to play the hero.

Bisnonna looked from Salvatore to Dave. She shuffled forward and stood protectively in front of Dave. Her cheeks were sunken in and she was trembling. Bloody Salvatore. Why did he have to ruin her night? Poor thing. I moved forward to pull Bisnonna out of the way. I didn't want her hurt if fists started flying.

Bisnonna raised her arthritic finger and pointed it at Salvatore, right into his face. '*Che tu Signore ti maledire.*'

Hell! Clutching Cami, I jumped clear of Bisnonna. *So much for poor thing.* I'd never seen Bisnonna throw a curse, but Daniella had told me she'd done it to her husband and how, once stricken with cancer, he'd begged her to let him die. I'd had so much bad luck since my marriage to Tony, I'd just assumed she'd cursed me too, but she'd never actually pointed her bony finger in my direction.

Bisnonna's dark eyes gleamed as she stared at Salvatore with such force, I swear I saw bolts of lightning leave her eyes. Okay, so that's an exaggeration, but that was how it felt to me.

Cami must have sensed something too, because her little fingers clutched my gown. 'Mamma!'

Salvatore's body went stiff, his eyes rolled back in his head and he dropped to the floor like a felled tree.

'What's happened?' Gia screamed, racing towards us.

'She cursed him,' I said. 'She's given him *iella*.' Bad luck.

'*Iella*? Oh no!' Gia wailed, her cry so loud that the music stopped and everyone turned to stare at Salvatore's prostrate body.

Lucy rushed over. 'What's happened?'

I did a double-take at Lucy. She had hundred dollar bills pinned all over her dress. 'You've been busy.'

'The men all insist on paying to dance with me. My dress is going to be full of pin holes. My mother's horrified.'

'You should have carried *la borsa*.' The money bag.

Salvatore groaned.

'Did he get into a fight?' Lucy asked.

'Bisnonna has put a curse on him,' I explained to her.

'Wow! She's better than mace,' Lucy said. She gazed at Bisnonna in awe.

Dave looked at me, bemused. 'Gabriella, you don't really believe in this stuff, do you?'

'Look at him,' I said, pointing to Salvatore. 'One minute he's standing, the next he's flattened.'

'Bisnonna really cross,' Cami said. 'Bye, bye, Salvatore.' She wiggled out of my arms and went to look more closely at him.

'Hee, hee, hee,' Bisnonna said. She tottered over to Salvatore and stood staring down at him, her orthopaedic shoes spread wide like a gunfighter's, her hands on her hips. Cami copied her stance.

'You are silly, Gabriella,' Dave said. 'He's drunk.' He bent down and tapped Salvatore on the face. 'Hey you, *cretino*, wake up.'

Salvatore groaned and opened his eyes. '*Malocchio,*' Evil Eye, he said to Bisnonna. He tried to rise but he couldn't. '*Sto male,*' I'm sick, he cried, clutching his stomach.

Gia started to wail until Riccardo hurried over.

'What's the matter?' Riccardo asked.

'Bisnonna cursed Salvatore,' Gia cried. 'Now I can never marry him. He's going to die. I have to start over.'

I looked around. Everyone was staring down at Salvatore and crossing themselves.

'I can't believe this,' Dave muttered, looking around him. He ran his fingers through his hair. 'Does everyone believe in *malocchio* here? What century do you people live in?'

'Bisnonna's husband died a terrible death,' I said to Dave. 'She has the Evil Eye. No one can afford to get on her wrong side.'

Dave shook his head. His arrogance irritated me.

Tony came over and squatted near Salvatore. 'She curse him?' he asked me.

I nodded.

'We'd better get Salvatore to a hospital,' Tony said, taking control. 'You, Gia, get your car. You drive. I'm over the limit.'

I grudgingly had respect for Tony in that moment. He might be crap in bed but he was good in an emergency. Effective. Masterful.

Tony and Riccardo hauled Salvatore to his feet, but he couldn't seem to walk. His eyes remained unfocused, his head lolled as if he'd broken his neck. Putting his arms around their necks, Tony and Riccardo dragged him outside and a tearful Gia, whinging about her lack of marriage prospects, followed behind.

'I can't believe this,' Dave said.

'You don't know everything,' I snapped. 'Okay, so *malocchio's* a Sicilian thing, but plenty of people here are from the north of Italy and they believe Bisnonna has The Eye.'

'Really?' Dave looked over at Bisnonna. '*Bisnonna. Che lei fa il malocchio?*' Bisnonna. Do you have the Evil Eye?

'Hee, hee, hee,' Bisnonna said. '*Non ti preoccupare, fidanzato.*' Don't you worry, fiancé, Bisnonna said, tottering over to him and taking his arm.

'I guess I'm safe,' Dave said.

I rolled my eyes. Dave put his free arm around my shoulder so that we stood there, Bisnonna, Dave and me–a discordant mixture of relationships. I figured with our age difference our relationship had as much chance of lasting as Dave and Bisnonna's.

'Don't worry. You are family. You're safe too,' Dave said.

'Bisnonna never wanted me to marry Tony,' I said quietly to him, so that Bisnonna couldn't hear.

'She's got good taste in men,' Dave said.

'Oh please.'

Dave grinned. 'So why did you?'

'I...I loved him.' I could feel a lump forming in my throat as I said those words out loud.

I watched as Tony held Salvatore up while Gia went to get the car. My gaze followed the sweep of his broad shoulders. He wasn't a tall man but he was strong. Cami was there saying something to him. He flashed our daughter a smile, perhaps telling her not to worry about Salvatore, reassuring her so that she didn't get upset.

I loved it when Tony smiled. He had brilliant white teeth and a big smile like Cary Grant's.

Dave gripped my arm tightly. 'It's time to go now.'

I looked at him startled. 'We can't go. The bride hasn't left.'

'I've had enough!'

Was Bisnonna driving Dave nuts by hanging off him? 'What do you mean?' Dave wasn't looking at me. Instead, he was staring at Tony.

The expression in Dave's eyes was hard; his mouth was turned down in a sulky line. 'I think you've put on a good enough show of getting on with your husband. His relatives will be impressed with how civilised you are.'

'I've barely talked to Tony,' I protested. 'Why are you suddenly so jealous?'

Dave scowled down at me. 'It's what you don't say that bothers me. It's the way you look at him.'

15

'Gabrrrriella, we need to talk,' Dave said as he took my house keys and opened the door for me.

Oh God, was I about to be unmasked? Did Dave know about our eleven-year age difference?

Who had betrayed me by telling Dave my age? Who'd had the opportunity? Daniella? Pino?

'Let me get Cami to bed,' I said. I pushed open Cami's bedroom door with my shoulder, took off her dress and tights and put her into her nightie. Luckily Cami, once asleep, generally stayed that way. I closed her door behind me.

I took a deep breath to steel myself. I knew this day would come. How I hated living on this knife's edge. I didn't like living a lie.

Dave walked into my bedroom instead of going down the hallway and settling into the living room. He took off his tuxedo jacket, flung it on the bed and sat with his arms folded.

Like the Tarantella, my life seemed to be a dance of discord. My stomach clenched. I'd never been a good liar. For a moment I thought about not turning on the bedroom light so that Dave couldn't see my guilt, but I knew I had to face my moment of truth. I wasn't proud that I had misled him about my age. I guess when we'd first met I hadn't expected much. I certainly hadn't expected him to fall in love with me.

I clicked on the light switch.

'What do you want to talk about?'

'You still love your husband.'

I saw Dave watching me intently, zeroing in on my face, not looking for age lines, but for my response. What he must have seen, however, was relief. I wasn't unmasked. I hadn't been caught out lying.

'Love Tony? We were together a long time. It isn't easy to stop caring. I'm sorry, I'm not trying to hurt you.'

I realised now that it hadn't been realistic to throw Tony out and think I could cauterise my feelings for him like a surgeon staunching a bleed. It took time for love to die, especially after a long relationship. I knew that in time any feelings I had left for him would wither, until he would mean nothing more to me other than being Cami's father. We'd discuss school reports and maintain civilised child access visits, our hearts dead for each other.

Dave came towards me, took me by the shoulders so that he could stare straight down into my eyes. 'I see the way he looks at you,' Dave persisted, his eyes alight with jealousy. 'I saw what he said to you at the altar. He loves you! You let him hold your hand as you walked down the aisle. How could you do that Gabrrrriella?'

Dave was working his way up to a full-on jealous-Italian tantrum. Placid Tony had never done them, so I'd never experienced one firsthand, except from my little brothers. I really wasn't in the mood for it. I'd had enough excitement for one night at the wedding. All I wanted to do was crawl into bed.

'Look, this is hard for me too, so quit pushing me,' I snapped.

'When I was a boy, my mother had other men,' Dave started.

'Not this again. I don't want to hear about it.' I pushed him away.

Dave grabbed me by the arm. 'My father let it happen because he couldn't bear to lose my mother. He let her cuckold him.' Dave gripped me by the arms. 'I am not like him.'

I didn't think this was the time to remind him that his father was not his genetic father.

'I don't like it that your husband still wants you.'

'Then maybe you should go.'

I fell into bed but I was unable to sleep. I tossed and turned feeling I had been cruel to Dave, yet I knew I wasn't in love with him. Whatever we had together was coming to an end. It was no more than a fling. Maybe affairs worked for other women, but for me, I realised it was no more than a quick fix.

I heard a knock on the door and groaned. Why wouldn't Dave leave me alone? I crawled out of bed and opened the door.

Tony stood on my doorstep.

'What are you doing here?'

'Please, Gabriella, I want to come home. I'm so unhappy without you. I walked down that aisle knowing you weren't mine. I couldn't bear it.'

My heart was in my mouth when he said those words. It had rubbed in our failure; ground it in like dirt on a wound.

'Where is he?' Tony asked.

I knew Tony meant Dave. 'Not here.'

Tony had his arms crossed over his stomach as if he were cold. 'Can I come in?'

I moved aside to let him pass. I noticed that Tony's face was drawn. He looked tired, emotionally wrung out, a mirror of myself. His shirt was open at the neck, his bow tie dangled from his pocket. I saw that his tuxedo jacket was creased at the back as he moved past me.

Tony stopped at my bedroom door. 'Has he spent the night in our room?'

'I'm not going to talk about my private life. Let me go Tony. We have to stop torturing each other.'

'I can't. I've loved you too much to let you go from my life. I can't give up. I'll always love you.' Tony couldn't help himself, he turned on my bedroom light and scanned the room, looking for changes, perhaps trying to sense if Dave had been there. He was haggard with pain and my heart went out to him.

'Come sit in the kitchen. I'll make you a hot drink.' I knew that Tony was in agony from the way he held his hand across his stomach. The cold often gave him crippling stomach cramps and it was chilly outside.

As he moved up the hallway, he stopped at Cami's room. 'Did you tell Cami about him?'

'I told her Dave's a friend. She's too young to understand more than that.'

Tony winced.

'It killed me to see you with him. I'll never stop loving you, Gabby. Please give us another chance.'

'I can't because nothing would change.'

When Tony is in pain his skin takes on a grey tinge. His cheeks looked hollowed out and he was black under his eyes. The state of him should have moved him, but I had grown tougher than I used to be and for that I was grateful. He hadn't made love to me for three years. I had begged him to. Literally begged him. 'I don't want the kind of marriage we had before. That's not good enough for me.'

I knew what it was like to be desired instead of taken for granted, and yet, oddly enough, for the first time in my life I wanted to be alone to think.

Tony's gaze roved over me, which gave me a funny sensation in the pit of my stomach. I mean we'd been together so long, I knew what it was like to be naked under my dressing gown in front of him. But this was different. It was if he were seeing me as a sexual being, imagining what I was like without my robe. It had been a long time since he'd looked at me like that.

I hurried up the hallway, past the living room and into the kitchen. I avoided his gaze. Instead I busied myself by taking out mugs and turning on the kettle.

Tony followed me into the kitchen, his hands held out beseechingly. 'You're my wife. I cheated on you. I was wrong to do that, but you have punished me enough. Please Gabby, can't we fix this? I don't want to lose you.'

For the first time, I heard the words I thought I would never hear from my husband. Genuine contrition. Tony finally felt my rejection the way I had felt his.

'You hurt me,' I said.

'I know.' Tony pulled me to him.

I pushed him away. 'You didn't want to touch me for three years. Do you know what that did to me?'

'It won't be like that again.' He grabbed my arm and pulled me close so that my breasts were pushed flat against his chest. I remembered how good it used to feel in his arms. We fitted together well. We always did.

It would have been so easy to relax into his arms. I could feel his heart thudding against mine, really hammering as if every bit of pain was expelling itself from his heart.

I put my hands on his chest and pushed away but Tony wouldn't let go. This close to him, I could smell his enticing cologne, feel his body heat. I wanted him to keep holding me, but I hated him too.

'I can't stand having a sexless marriage. Do you have any idea how cruel that was? You starved me of sex while you went with

Betty. I felt rotten when I was with you. I thought it was my fault but I know now it's not. Dave tells me how beautiful I am. He makes me feel desirable.'

Tony looked like I'd slapped him.

I felt his body tense against mine, but he didn't let me go, no matter how harsh my words.

'He's right. You are beautiful, Gabriella.'

This was so unlike Tony. I couldn't believe he was talking to me and blaming himself. For once there wasn't the impenetrable wall–the no-go-zones of communication, that tore our marriage apart. This was the first time since the birth of Cami that he didn't fob me off by telling me he didn't want to talk or look at me as I was *pazzo*. Crazy. Tony was desperate for me and maybe that would have turned other women off, but not me. I wanted to see him express his real feelings instead of hiding them like he always did.

The anger in me faded.

Tony bent his head and kissed me. I shouldn't have let him kiss me, but I liked the feel of his arms around me and his warm lips on mine.

In the background, I could hear the kettle coming to the boil behind me. There was steam rising over Tony's head, clouding the air, just as my thoughts were clouded.

Tony took my hand and did something he hadn't done in years. He took my hand and put it on his crotch.

He was hard.

I looked at him, surprised. I'd had plenty of false starts in the three years since Cami's birth when Tony couldn't maintain an erection. I didn't think I could bear another.

'You've got an erection?'

'I want you. Can't you feel how much I desire you?'

I pulled my hand away. 'Don't do this to me.'

'I love you.'

I struggled out of his grip. 'Stop saying that. I don't want to hear it. I told you I need more than emotional love. I need the physical too.'

Once I would have been happy to have him say those words to me, but not any more. It was doing my head in.

'Please Gabby, don't shut me out.' He moved towards me so that I was backed up against the kitchen counter.

I slapped my hands against his chest so that he couldn't pull me close, but he pulled me in by the hips so that we were joined. I could feel him throbbing against me.

'I've replaced you and you don't like it. That's what's bothering you. It's bruised your Italian male ego. Why don't you just accept that we're finished?'

'I know you still love me. I saw it in your eyes at the church. You've never been good at hiding your feelings.'

'I do love you, but I'm stronger now. I'd been thinking about leaving you for a long time because of our problems. Your affair was the catalyst.'

'We've had twenty tears together. Don't throw them away.' Tony slid his arm around the back of my neck and kissed me again.

The trouble was, I always responded to my husband's touch. I didn't want to like it, but his kiss was passionate and hot like when we'd first met. I didn't want to feel for him, but that damn man had an emotional hold on me that was difficult to break. I couldn't slice a twenty-year relationship out of my life so easily. All the sexual frustration that had tormented me rose up at that moment as I kissed Tony back.

I sank into the kiss, my tongue teasing his.

Tony pushed my robe from my shoulders so that it slid down my body, leaving me naked under the moonlight.

'I can't stand to think of any man's hands on you but mine.'

No matter that Dave's touch was new and fresh, I loved my husband. It felt so good to be in his arms again.

Tony pulled the sleeves of his jacket off so that it fell to the floor with a soft thud. His hands were trembling with desperation as if he couldn't get enough of me. He kissed and stroked my breasts like he had never seen them before.

When he played with my breasts I felt my clitoris pulse.

This was what I'd wanted from him for so long. I should have said no. Dave didn't deserve this. I should have held back, but I wanted to feel my husband inside of me. I had wanted him to make love to me for so long that I couldn't stop myself.

I pulled Tony's belt and unzipped him. I was so determined to have him I didn't care whether he was undressed or not.

Tony picked me up and placed me on the kitchen bench. He spread my thighs wide, opening me to him.

'You don't know how much I've wanted you.'

My nipples were hot, pointy coals. I leaned back so that my throat was exposed. Everything about me was completely open. This was so right. This was what I needed.

Every ounce of my being wanted him, wanted things to be good again, wanted his cock. Tony didn't waste any time, he slid in to me, thrusting deeply.

I closed my eyes and sighed with pleasure. This felt so right. He slid one hand around the back of my hips and teased my clitoris with the other. I bucked involuntarily. All the frustration that had built inside me released into a series of orgasms that flooded through me. I arched into him, writhing and thrusting while he bit down on my nipples.

It was wild animal sex made of pure desperation.

I heaved in big gulps of air as my orgasms subsided. Tony was still inside me. All the love that I had crushed down in anger flowed through me at that moment. I stared into his face but Tony wasn't looking at me.

His eyes were glazed. His face was puce. He pushed himself away from me, clutching at his heart. 'Help me, Gabby. I'm in pain.'

'What's happening?'

'My heart,' he gasped. 'Pain. Terrible pain.'

'Oh my God. I'll call an ambulance.' I jumped off the kitchen bench, but my legs were wobbly and I nearly fell. I caught the kitchen bench to recover then ran for the phone which was mounted on the kitchen wall.

When Pino was in his forties he'd had a heart attack, so chest pain was taken seriously in Tony's family. Tonight had been a night of unbelievable stress for both of us. I know my heart felt pulled in two.

Fingers trembling, I dialled 000 and prayed. I begged the operator to send an ambulance quickly. Under the moonlight, I could see the amulets I had hung on my wall, glinting. Was this part of Bisnonna's curse? She'd never wanted me in the family. Surely she wouldn't kill her own grandson to get rid of me?

I turned to Tony. He was lying on the floor clutching his heart.

I got to my knees beside him and prayed. 'Please God, don't let him die.'

I didn't think God would listen to me any more. I was certain the doors of heaven were closed to me forever. Why did he have to take my husband just when we had a chance to be together again?

16

'You're here again, Mr Vitadini. I thought you'd be sick of this place,' the doctor in the emergency room of North Shore hospital said to Tony. I saw by his badge he was Dr Graph.

I looked around the whitewashed walls of the room, taking in the scuff marks on the walls, the smell of disinfectant. I couldn't believe I was there. I gave Tony's hand a squeeze to reassure him, even though I wasn't feeling all that positive myself.

Tony gave me a watery smile. 'I brought Salvatore here,' he explained.

I'd forgotten to ask about Salvatore, but at the moment Tony's health was more important to me. I couldn't believe my strong husband was lying on a gurney. He'd barely had a sick day in his life.

'Must have been some wedding you went to,' DrGraph said. 'Your buddy is still here under observation. Can't work out what's wrong with him.'

'Can you unbutton your shirt?' Dr Graph asked Tony.

'Here, I'll do it.' I quickly unbuttoned Tony's white shirt so that the doctor could listen to his heartbeat. I watched the doctor's face as he listened. He frowned, wheeled over the blood pressure machine and took Tony's blood pressure.

'That's elevated.' His gaze flicked over to me and back to Tony. 'You looked fine when you came in earlier. What have you been up to?'

Vigorous sex on the kitchen bench. I couldn't say that, not even to a doctor. I closed my fingers into a fist as I looked at Tony. My nails dug into my palm. *This was all my fault.* I'd driven Tony to breaking point. I'd kicked him out of his home, humiliated him in front of his family and friends. What if he died? How would I ever explain that to Cami? How would I ever look Pino and Daniella in the face?

'Trying to make my wife happy,' Tony said.

'Overdoing it, I'd say,' said the doctor, taking a quick glance at me.

Blood rushed to my cheeks in embarrassment.

My mother always told me everything I did would show on my face.' Are you nauseated, do you have pain, numbness, tingling in your chest?' Dr Graph asked Tony.

'My heart is thumping.' Tony put his hand on his heart area. Then he did something that surprised me. He pointed to his groin. 'I'm in pain there too.'

I stared to where he pointed. It was clearly evident that Tony still had an erection. His penis, constrained by his black trousers, was pointing slightly to the left like the Leaning Tower of Pisa.

'What have you taken?' the doctor asked.

'N...Nothing.' Tony looked at me, his eyes wide with alarm.

Couldn't the doctor see that Tony was having a heart attack? I hadn't gone to med school but it seemed obvious to me. I'd got him to hospital alive and well enough to communicate. Couldn't the doctor just get on with it?

I took Tony's hand and gave it another comforting squeeze. We were good together in an emergency. 'Look doctor, Tony's family has a history of heart problems. His father had a heart attack at forty. It's in his genes.'

The doctor gave me a speculative look. What was he thinking? Okay, so I wasn't looking my best. I'd pulled on a long-sleeved blue cotton top and jeans. I hadn't even had time to put on my bra and I was sure that the outline of my nipples could be seen through the top. It wasn't such a big deal, was it?

Did I look tarty?

Was my Catholic guilt overwhelming?

I could hardly be expected to look good in the early hours of the morning, what with calling the ambulance, waking up my neighbour to mind Cami and rushing off with Tony to the hospital.

Why was the doctor staring at me in that weird way?

'It isn't normal to have a heart attack and maintain an erection,' the doctor said to me at last.

Huh? It was kind of weird. I looked at Tony's tower again. Yep. Still up. I frowned. All these years I'd wanted him to be amorous with me and now his erection was an embarrassment. Why here? Why now? Life sucked.

I stared at Tony's contorted face. Guilt ate at me until my insides twisted. I'd caused this heart attack. This was my fault. 'Please, Dr Graph, give my husband something to stop the pain.'

The doctor persisted with his questions. 'Mr Vitadini, tell me what you've taken.'

Tony looked at me and back to the doctor. Beads of perspiration formed on his brow.

Although his eyes were bloodshot, I knew Tony never touched drugs. Tony was anti drugs. He wouldn't even take a headache tablet. What was this doctor on about? I could feel a scream welling up in my throat.

He was going to die just when our marriage had hope. Tony was sorry. He loved me again. He'd proved he found me desirable. Even the fabulous sex with Dave hadn't stopped me loving Tony. Without love, sex was hollow. Dave didn't suit me the way Tony did.

I glared at the doctor.

'Mr Vitadini, if you won't come clean with me, I can't help you,' the doctor said. 'How long have you had this painful erection?'

'T...three hours,' Tony stuttered.

Three hours? He'd only been with me for an hour and a half. What had he been doing with it the rest of the time? Playing with it? Admiring it? I'd never known Tony to last that long.

'You do realise that you can have permanent damage to your penis if your erection lasts more than six hours,' the doctor said. 'Please cooperate with me or I can't treat you.'

Tony blanched so that there was no colour left in his face. He looked like the corpse he was about to become.

'I've taken Viagra,' Tony said, his voice so quiet I had to lean forward to hear him.

'Huh?' I looked from Tony to the doctor and back again.

Tony was staring straight at me. Stricken.

I stared between his legs.

The doctor had known all along. No wonder he'd looked at me strangely as I carried on about Pino's history of heart problems. This wasn't the same thing at all.

'I think you're having some sort of reaction. Is this the first time you've taken it?' Dr Graph asked.

Tony nodded, but he wasn't looking at the doctor, he was staring straight at me, his eyes wide with alarm.

The volcano that lived inside me boiled over. I snatched my hand away from Tony's. 'You needed Viagra to have sex with me?' I screamed.

'Please Mrs Vitadini. You're distressing your husband,' the doctor admonished me.

'You didn't need it for Betty, did you? Just me!' My hand went to my heart. 'Your wife!'

'I'm sorry, Gabby. I tried my best. I couldn't. I just couldn't-'

'That was your best?' Hands on hips, I leaned over Tony. 'You bastard,' I spat into his face. 'You wanted to break up my relationship with Dave, didn't you?'

Tony got off the gurney and clutched my hand. 'I'm your husband. You shouldn't be with him,' he said, his voice hoarse with pain.

'It's all about ego for you, isn't it? You couldn't stand to see me happy with someone else. You couldn't bear it, that I replaced you.'

Tony groaned.

The doctor came towards me. 'Mrs Vitadini. I want you to leave,' he ordered. 'Upsetting your husband will not help his condition.'

'He's not my husband. He's a lying, Viagra-using cheat.'

I looked past the doctor, straight into Tony's eyes. 'I'm finished with you.'

I tried to shake my hand free from his, but he had me in a grip so hard I literally had to peel his hand from mine.

'Don't leave me, Gabby,' he pleaded.

I ran out of the hospital, tears streaming from my eyes. I'd said so many times that I wasn't going back to Tony, but that was anger talking. Deep inside, past the turmoil of betrayal, I'd wanted to save my marriage. I couldn't escape my upbringing no matter how hard I tried.

I'd genuinely believed Tony was sorry for his infidelity. When he'd made love to me, with such passion, I'd thought it came from the heart instead of from a pill.

To turn up on my doorstep in the dead of night, to beg to come in and to behave like he still loved me, of course I'd fallen for it.

I fell for it because I hated having my family torn apart, but more than that, when I'd made love to Tony it had come from my heart.

What a sad, sad, joke.

All my hopes for finding some way to save my marriage were dashed. Tony cheated on me. His attempt to make love to me was no more than a lie.

But what was I?

I wasn't any different. I'd barely pushed Dave out the door before Tony had come in. Dave, who really loved me, and wanted to make a future with me. I lied to Dave about my age. I was no better than Tony. I was a liar and a cheat.

How could I look Dave in the face? I couldn't even look at myself in the mirror.

17

I wore dark glasses into work that morning to hide the redness of my eyes. I'd spent the early hours of the morning crying my eyes out in the shower, so that the sounds of my grief wouldn't wake Cami.

I couldn't seem to pull myself together, so I kept a bundle of tissues under the cuff of the crisp black shirt I was wearing, just in case the tears streamed over again. I'd matched my shirt with a black skirt and jacket. The look was funereal to suit my mood. I hoped no one in the office would examine my face because no amount of make-up could hide the puffy edges around my eyes.

Muttering a good morning to the new receptionist, I made a beeline to my desk, sat and looked with blurry vision at my computer screen to check my appointments. I had a new client booked in to see the Temple at nine. I glanced at my watch. I had twenty minutes to compose myself.

I heard the familiar click of high heels coming towards me. I usually called a cheery hello to Christine on the way in, but I'd avoided my boss this morning.

'Good morning, Christine.' I didn't look up, because I knew

that Christine, who was good at reading me, would want to know what was going on.

Christine stopped at my desk. 'Good morning, Gabriella. When you have a moment, I need to see you in my office.'

'No problem.' I looked up at my boss briefly, so as not to be rude. She was wearing a striking turquoise suit with a silver Tiffany necklace, and gorgeous Emma Hope shoes that I lusted after. The ensemble looked terrific with her blonde bob. Very cheerful.

We couldn't have looked more different. I hadn't even bothered with my usual gold jewellery. I couldn't find the energy to adorn myself with a necklace, nor the dangly gold earrings I usually wore.

'I'll be free for half an hour after this next appointment,' I said, staring back at my computer, pretending to check my screen. *Please don't comment on my ravaged face.*

'Dark glasses inside? Big night last night?'

'You know Italian weddings,' I mumbled. 'They go on forever.' Things were just great. Not!

Christine stood beside my desk looking at me. I glanced up at her again to see what more she wanted. There was an expression in her eyes I hadn't seen before. A hardness. Dislike?

Don't get me wrong, when chasing the almighty dollar Christine was one tough cookie, but this was different. She was staring down at me with her eyes narrowed like I was dirt under her fingernails. What was eating her? Jeez, I didn't need this right now. All I wanted to do was throw myself into my work and try to forget that my life was unravelling.

'Excuse me, Christine. I need a bathroom stop.' I quickly got up from my desk before she could converse with me any more and hurried into the bathroom. Taking off my glasses, I bathed my puffy eyes, pulled my compact out of my handbag and powdered my face again. I dug out my latest Revlon lipstick and put it on. I hoped the crimson slash of colour would draw attention away from my eyes. They were still swollen and red around the lids.

In the harsh light of the bathroom I examined myself, knowing I wouldn't like what I saw. Try as I might, I couldn't escape my Catholic-Italian roots. I had to look at myself. I swear I'd aged ten years last night. I looked every one of my forty years, instead of the thirty or so that Dave believed me to be. There were lines under my eyes and fine dehydration lines on my forehead that hadn't been there before. Even my cheeks looked puffy and bloated as if I'd been drinking.

I looked a mess.

It was hardly surprising considering the stress I was under. I hated Tony. But even hatred hadn't stopped me phoning the hospital every hour to check up on his progress. Why did this man still have power over me?

I wanted to move on. I really did. I had a terrific guy who cared for me, yet last night I couldn't get him out the door fast enough. Poor Dave would be horrified to know that I'd been with Tony. He was right when he'd said I was still in love with my husband even though the situation was hopeless.

My wan face stared back at me. I quickly applied more blush. I knew I couldn't tell Dave what I'd done, but I couldn't live with my deception either.

My betrayal would be yet another piece of dishonesty lying between us.

What kind of relationship could grow from that? Dave deserved better.

'The Temple apartments are selling fast,' I said to my client Mr Boyd, who was pushing seventy and his trophy wife, Vanessa. The dress she wore looked like it had been sewn on, but I had to say it suited her sleek brunette looks and hour-glass figure. I wondered how Mr Boyd had met her.

MrBoyd stared upwards at the ceiling. I swear he would have poked it with his walking stick if his back had been straight enough to reach. *Had bonking Mrs Boyd put his back out?*

'Pity the penthouse is gone. I don't like the idea of hearing people above me,' he wheezed. He gave a hacking cough.

Stuffed into Mr Boyd's ear, surrounded by sprouting grey hair was a hearing aid, but I didn't think it was tactful to point that out.

'The apartment is soundly built. You won't have a problem with noise,' I said with confidence. If I made this sale, it would be my fourth including Dave's in the past two weeks. I was on a roll.

I loved my job. Selling gave me a high. Apart from Cami, it was the best thing in my life at the moment, the only thing I didn't feel guilty about. I put everything I could into this job.

'I like this place. It's very classy. The living room is enormous. I can fit the equipment we need to make you comfortable in here,' Mrs Boyd said to her husband.

Equipment? What did she do to him? Come to think of it, a rack would straighten his old back out.

'What do you do, Mrs Boyd?' Okay, I admit it. I was as nosy as Gia. I couldn't help myself. Blame it on the age difference of at least thirty years in the couple in front of me. It was, after all, a subject that I found compelling.

'I'm a nurse. That's how we met.' She gave her husband a squeeze and his face lit up in a smile. 'Arthur's health has taken a turn for the worse. I'm going to set up a room as good as any hospital, so that Arthur has everything he needs.'

Oh, I would go to hell for my dirty mind.

Mr Boyd coughed.

I looked from one to the other. 'That's really nice.' From the sound of his cough, I hoped Arthur lived long enough to enjoy this apartment if he bought it.

Mrs Boyd took her husband by the arm. 'Come on lover, let's see the bedroom.'

I watched open-mouthed as Mrs Boyd's unlikely lover hobbled into the master bedroom. Was she planning on bonking him to death to hasten his departure to the next world? I had a mental picture of Tony lying on the hospital gurney. Who was I to judge these people?

My dialling finger itched to phone the hospital again. What a *casino.* A mess.

I followed Mrs Boyd into the bedroom, watching her as she opened and closed the doors to the built-in cupboards. What was this bombshell doing with Arthur? How could she stand to have sex with him?

Mrs Boyd saw me assessing her.

Oops!

Her eyes narrowed. 'I know what you're thinking,' she said.

'Pardon?'

'You think he's too old for me, don't you?'

Oh God, how embarrassing. Arthur turned to look at me too. My cheeks flamed. 'I...I...I...' How could I deny it? I *was* thinking that. My mother was right. Everything showed on my face. 'I, er...um, am actually going out with someone myself. There's quite an age gap, too. I was wondering how you coped. I'm so sorry if you picked up on that. I didn't mean to be impolite.'

Mrs Boyd's face softened. 'I'm sorry I snapped at you. It's hard sometimes. The way people stare at us. Someone even asked me if I was a hooker once.'

'How rude!'

'It makes me mad. I guess I get defensive. I'm sure you understand though.'

'I think you're strong. Brave. I'm not comfortable with the age difference.'

Mrs Boyd's face lit up. 'New relationship?'

'I don't think it will last.'

'You'll find age doesn't make any difference when you love someone. I've nursed Arthur for years. It is possible to fall in love with an older man. Arthur's so kind to me, so patient. I'm much happier with him than anyone else. Is it like that for you?'

'Er, sort of.' *Not!*

Oh God, was I going to be like that when people looked at Dave and me? Defensive? I wouldn't always look this young, not with these stress wrinkles appearing. Sure, there wasn't the age gap that these two had, but eleven years was eleven years.

'Oh, will you look at this, lover.' Mrs Boyd waltzed over to the picture window. 'There's a fantastic view from this room too. Look how the Opera House is covered in fog. I can see the city though.'

'It's very expensive, honey,' Mr Boyd complained.

'You can afford it. You've worked hard all your life. We're not skimping on anything at this point. You deserve the best. Besides, I've never had a bedroom with a marble bath.' Mrs Boyd turned to me with a smile. 'That is marble, isn't it?'

'Calacatta.' I knew my stone thanks to Dave. Gorgeous Dave — the man who had taught me to feel confident about my desirability again. I owed him big time and yet, my heart wasn't with him, no matter how much I wanted it to be.

I tried to shake the disgruntled look he'd given me when I'd almost pushed him out of my house last night. Had I destroyed that relationship too?

'This apartment looks well built,' Mrs Boyd said.

'The Temple has the best finishes,' I said, kicking back into work mode. 'The developer hasn't cut corners. This is a most prestigious establishment. There's also a gym, spa and pool downstairs.'

Nine times out of ten, the woman makes the decision to buy a home and it seemed to me that Mrs Body, er, Mrs Boyd was calling the shots here.

God, hope old Mr Boyd didn't overdo it in the spa. Hate to think of him boiling away there.

'We'll take it,' Mrs Boyd said.

'But Honey Bear,' Mr Boyd protested, 'we have to negotiate.'

'We don't have time to muck about,' Mrs Boyd said. 'You know that.'

Mr Boyd gave me a weak smile. He coughed so hard he nearly lost balance. 'She wants it. I want to make her happy.'

Would it be like that for me if I stayed with Dave? Would I look like an old woman trying to please my young stud? When he was thirty nine, I would be fifty. I'd look a lot older than him then. Would people stare at us and think Dave was a hooker paid to keep me happy?

I couldn't bear to think about it.

I showed Mr and Mrs Boyd into Christine's office so that they could do the paperwork for the apartment.

'You've done the right thing,' my boss said to our clients. 'Most people want to look at an apartment several times, but then they miss out. The Temple is selling fast.' Christine smiled so wide, I could see her pointy eye-teeth glistening as she put the contract in front of the Boyds.

She didn't acknowledge me or tell me what great selling work I'd done. Normally, she'd give me a friendly nudge and congratulations.

What had I done?

I hoped this sale would put her in a better mood for

whatever she wanted to discuss with me because she was behaving strangely.

After the Boyds had paid a deposit and signed their contract, I showed them out onto Martin Place.

A blast of noise hit me from the street. Traffic and people smells assaulted my senses, but I wanted to step outside the office for a moment.

When I shook my clients' hands goodbye–Vanessa's soft one and Arthur's crinkly old one–I reminded myself to use more moisturizer on my own hands so that they didn't age so fast.

Somehow, Mrs Boyd had managed to overcome any issues so that their age difference didn't bother her. What was wrong with me? Why couldn't I move on from Tony to Dave and be happy that I had such a great young guy in love with me?

Was it my culture stopping me?

I mean, in my culture in generations past, people of different ages did marry. Naturally, the older person was always the man. Men liked a younger wife because they considered a younger woman more fertile. Even now, none of my Italian-Australian girlfriends were with men younger than them.

I was breaking the mould.

I wasn't comfortable with my situation.

I looked at my watch. In my left hand, I carried my mobile phone like it was a third limb. I couldn't help it. Despite my anger and hurt at Tony, I still wanted to know how he was doing. I couldn't bear to think of him alone in hospital. I knew he wouldn't call his parents because of the shame attached to his situation. Pino, the great philanderer, would be horrified if he found out that his son needed Viagra to make love to his wife. No doubt, he would find some way to blame the problem on me if he found out.

I dialled the hospital to inquire about Tony's health.

'I can put you through to him,' the over-helpful receptionist said.

'No. That's okay. I prefer to speak to the doctor.' Unfortunately, I didn't get time to finish my sentence before she transferred the call.

'Hello?' Tony said.

For a moment I wanted to hang up. I hesitated. 'H...hi. It's Gabby.' It hurt even to talk to Tony. Every time I talked to him, the reminder of how sexually inadequate he made me feel hit me in the guts. I had to keep reminding myself that the fault didn't lie with me.

So why did I bother to check up on him? I guess I wasn't a cruel person. That thread that had held us together for so long was still there, be it tenuous and frayed. Why couldn't we get the passion back that we'd had? Tony was Cami's father and I had to know that the father of my child was not in danger.

I'd screamed at Tony when he'd been his most vulnerable. I'd deserted him in the hospital when he needed me most. I thought back to the Clinic, where I had been so alone with my little baby, where no one in the family had visited me because I'd had a mental illness, but Tony had stuck by me then. I knew how painful it was to be discarded, to have the wrong illness, the wrong type of problem.

I wasn't proud of walking away from him that night.

'Gabby?' Tony asked. 'Is that really you?' He sounded so pleased to hear from me.

My heart caught in my throat, so that I could barely speak. The rush of emotions caught me unprepared. 'Are...are you all right?'

'I think so. The doctor wants to check on me again. My heart has stopped hammering.'

'And the other thing?' I couldn't even bring myself to say the word penis.

'It's going to be okay.'

'That will make you happy.' I didn't want to talk about it. I didn't want to think about his damned fake erection that still didn't work properly–at least not with me. It just made me too unhappy.

'I'm glad you're out of danger.' I managed to keep my voice steady. 'I couldn't bear to tell Cami you were sick. It would upset her. She's had enough disruption already.'

'That's not why you're ringing. I know you still love me, Gabby,' Tony confronted me. 'Dr Graph told me you called and asked about me every hour.'

A motorbike backfired in front of me, making me jump. The thick smell of petrol fumes made me gag. I could feel my own heart thumping. I moved closer to my office door. 'I have to go.'

'Damn it. Don't hang up on me, Gabby. I love you.'

I closed my mobile phone and pushed open my office door. How was it that my husband could tell me he loved me after being with Betty? I just didn't get it.

Then I thought about Dave when I'd so readily had sex with Tony too. Understanding dawned on me-Dave I didn't care about, not the way I did Tony, yet I'd still managed to make love to him and enjoy it.

Yet, in these last three weeks since I'd decided to put myself first, I was the unhappiest that I'd ever been. I wanted a promotion–I went for it, even though my work hours meant more time away from Cami; I wanted Dave and I was prepared to lie to have him and, consumed by lust, I'd had sex with Tony too. Being a liar and a cheat didn't sit comfortably on my shoulders because that wasn't my true nature.

I walked into the office to face Christine, determined to fix whatever was bothering her. I was good at my job and proud of it. God knows, I needed to feel good about something right now.

I knocked at Christine's door.

My boss was looking over the contract with a sour expression on her face. After a sale, she would usually be nodding and smiling at the thought of more money walking in the door.

Normally, clients pushed for a discount, but Mrs Boyd didn't bother, insisting only that nothing delay the sale because she wanted to get into the Temple as fast as possible.

The lack of argy bargy should have made Christine ecstatic. Instead, I could see that the sides of her mouth were turned down as if she'd eaten something unpleasant. My boss raised her head when I knocked. She frowned.

'Come in, Gabriella, and take a seat. Close the door behind you.'

A shiver went through me. Had one of my clients complained about something? I couldn't think what I could have done to upset anyone. I put everything I had into this job.

I did as Christine asked and sat in front of her.

'I'll get straight to the point, Gabriella. You've made a lot of sales for someone so new to this business. Are you sleeping with clients?'

A whoosh of blood shot to my face. I thought of old Mr Boyd and his wife. Had Christine gone mad? 'What are you suggesting? That I'm bonking old men and their wives? That's disgusting!'

'I don't know what to think, Gabriella, especially of you, of all people. I've never had any problem with you in the past. You've always been a steady, reliable worker. I've never doubted your character in any way. But since your marriage broke up...'

Shaking her head, she let that phrase hang in the air, but I wasn't touching that one. No way!

Had Tony rung the office and said something? He was determined to get rid of Dave, but he didn't have a mean character. It couldn't be that. Even though I'd kicked him out, he still insisted on covering the mortgage and the bills that he usually paid. Most men wouldn't do that.

I watched transfixed as Christine opened the top drawer of her desk and pulled out a brown envelope. She slit the envelope and fished out a pair of lacy underpants, holding them between her perfectly manicured index finger and thumb.

I felt the colour drain from my face, just as quickly as its whoosh of arrival. I recognised the underwear. They were the ones that Dave had kept as a memento. They must have fallen out of his pocket.

'Are these yours?'

I'm ashamed to admit, a lie came to my mouth more quickly than the truth. Everything was falling down around me at the moment, my relationship with Dave was scratchy, not to mention my failed marriage. I needed this job. How would I support Cami and myself without it? I wasn't going to ask Tony for money even though he'd happily help me.

'Of course they're not.'

I fought the expression of shock, which I'm sure I wore on my face, by changing it to indignation. Though, from the trembling feeling going on inside my body, I don't know how successful I was.

'No one has that key to the lift except this office,' Christine said, pointing her finger at me to drive her point home.

'What about the developer?' I shot back.

'He's in Europe at the moment.' Christine's eyes narrowed at my sassy tone.

What was happening to me? Even I didn't like my bitch mouth, but I was desperate.

Christine lips tightened. She pressed on. 'You went to the Temple with Mr Angelo and came back looking...'

Like a *puttana*. A whore.

'Dishevelled,' Christine said. 'When you and Mr Angelo were outside the office, I even saw...'

Oh, don't mention the pubic hair in his teeth. Spare me that!

'That Mr Angelo's zipper was undone.'

Not good, but less skanky than the pubic hair.

'Was it?' I'd missed that, but then I don't know how I'd even walked back to the office that day, the way my head had been in the clouds. It certainly wasn't now, though. I had to fight for my job.

I sat up straight, throwing my shoulders back. 'I saw the underwear in the elevator when I entered it with Mr Angelo. I remember kicking them into the corner. I didn't want to pick them up in front of him.'

'How would they get there?' Christine was clearly not convinced by my lies, but what could she do, DNA test the underwear?

I couldn't stand this. I hated lying to Christine. I felt dirty inside like some low-life creature crawling out of a bog. I wanted to talk to Christine. She was a nice boss who had given me a chance, but I knew from the disgust on her face that she would fire me.

I had to keep this job. I would break into a thousand pieces if I lost it.

I stood, shoving the chair away from my legs. 'I find your allegations insulting. If you're going to fire me, then do it, otherwise I'm going to get on with doing what I'm paid to do, selling real estate.'

Christine stared at me, with a hard expression on her face. 'I don't know what's happened to you, Gabriella, but you've changed. I don't like who you've become. You're not the same person I hired two years ago. You're not even the same person you were three weeks ago.'

And wasn't that the truth.

18

When I closed my eyes to go to sleep that night, I kept seeing Christine's face filled with disgust. She knew me for what I was. A liar. Now that she had caught me out in a lie, she would never trust me again.

That's how it was with liars. They gradually lost the love of the ones close to them and the trust of those they worked with. In the end, no one wanted to be around them and they ended up lonely and alone. A pariah in their own community.

When I was a child, I remember my mother pointing out a woman who'd had an affair. When her husband confronted her about the affair, she had lied about it. Her deceit had horrified my mother, but there was worse to come. The woman walked away from her marriage and left her children with her husband. This was something unheard of in my Italian-based culture.

My mother called her a liar and adulterer.

My father called her a *puttana*. Prostitute.

From my child's point of view, I couldn't imagine a mother leaving her family, unless death pulled her from their loving arms which, in my mother's case, it did.

I remember feeling my mother's hand tightening on mine, as

she pulled me past this woman in the street, not greeting her, even though they had known each other for twenty years, even though they had come from the same *paese*, the same village in Sicily.

That woman wore the face of shame.

After all I'd done recently, I recognised the look of shame on that woman's face on my own.

It was Saturday evening and I stood holding Cami's hand, at the door of Daniella and Pino's house. Cami held Bacci's lead. The dog sniffed the air and wagged her tail with excitement. My in-laws were so welcoming that they always had food, even for the dog.

Before I knocked, I could smell the tempting aroma of Pino's delicious spaghetti bolognese. My stomach rumbled. I took a deep breath. It smelled like Pino was cooking quail, with porcini mushroom too.

Knowing Pino, he would have cooked up a big saucepan of polenta to go with the quail, let it firm, then sliced it and put it under the grill so that it came out like a hot cornbread. It was delicious with Stracchino cheese. I could imagine my plate laden with the quail and polenta, *insalata* made of radicchio, a type of lamb's tongue lettuce, and borlotti beans cooked up in Pino's rich tomato and onion sauce.

I wasn't part of the family now.

Perhaps sensing my hesitation, Cami knocked on the door.

The door opened. Pino stood there with Tony, who had called me on Friday afternoon to say he had been discharged from hospital. A cheerful welcoming light shone from inside the house, illuminating the doorstep.

'*Buona sera*,' Pino said.

Cami ran into her father's arms, kissed him and then kissed

and hugged Pino. Bacci bounded forward too, running around Pino and Tony before settling to smell Pino's hands in the hope of a bone.

I stood there.

'Would you like to come in, Gabby?' Tony asked. Cami ran over and pulled at my hand. 'Come on, Mamma.'

I'd wanted to say yes at that moment. I wanted to ask Tony how he was feeling because he still looked a bad colour to me, although he had assured me he was better on the phone the day before.

Sure, I was still angry about him and Betty, but I had done so much these last few weeks that I wasn't proud of and that, somehow, had tempered my anger. Tony wasn't perfect, but nor was I.

I wanted to hear the family's chatter and laughter around me because I knew it would reinvigorate me, the way it so often did. Lucy had told me that she and Riccardo were invited too which would make the evening extra special; everyone would be discussing the wedding.

Lucy and Tony were bringing over Italian travel brochures because Riccardo wanted to talk with Pino and Daniella about where to stay in Venice. He was taking Lucy there for their honeymoon. I'd always wanted to go to Venice, but Tony and I had spent so much time working to get the size of our mortgage manageable that we had never done such a special trip.

I stared at Tony. He gave me a small smile. Maybe we should have. Maybe doing something so special together as walking hand in hand in the City of Love would have helped our marriage. It had certainly needed the romance, instead of all the hard work. Was that what had killed Tony's passion?

Daniella came to the door. She'd had fresh blonde highlights put in her hair and she looked pretty.

'Hello, Gabriella,' Daniella said. She didn't invite me in.

Instead, she came out to give me the customary kiss of greeting. Her cheek was soft on mine and her perfume familiar.

I looked into her eyes. I could see sadness there. I had broken up her son's marriage. There would always be sadness and disapproval in her eyes when she looked at me. Daniella once told me that she wouldn't have a divorced woman at her table. Although Daniella had suffered Pino's infidelity, she hadn't left.

Bacci nudged Daniella's hand and she smiled at the dog. 'Come on, Bacci.'

My dog would always be welcome at their home.

'Come in, Mamma,' Cami insisted. She came back to me and tugged at my hand, determined to get me across their stoop. Her little face turned red with exertion. She had never known a time when I hadn't joined the family.

I squatted. 'I can't darling. I'll pick you up after Mass tomorrow and we'll spend all day together.' I hugged my daughter to me then handed her to Tony and walked away.

My eyes burned with tears, but I didn't want anyone to see. I had made the decision to end my marriage so quickly that I hadn't thought about what it would cost me emotionally.

I was used to being a member of a large Italian family. My own in Brisbane and Tony's in Sydney.

I didn't like being alone. I wasn't good at it. I stood outside their house looking in at the happiness there.

My chest contracted with pain.

I was an outsider in a family I loved being part of, but I had to go through this if I was ever going to find my own way.

When Dave came to pick me up in his black Porsche on Saturday night, I got a kick when I saw him even though I knew I wanted to end it. He wore a wide smile, which showed his pleasure in seeing me.

No one, apart from Cami, greeted me with such enthusiasm any more.

Dave strode up my pathway, his dark hair flying in the cold night air. He wore a black, three-quarter leather coat, a crisp white shirt underneath, tight black jeans and pointy leather boots. As usual, he looked like he had stepped out of Italian Vogue. Except the Italian Vogue models didn't carry the penetrating 'fuck me' look that Dave had in his eyes.

'Gabrrrriella.' He pulled me into his arms and pressed his lips to mine, kissing me like he'd never see me again. His passion didn't move me the way it had a couple of weeks ago, but I realised how angry and self-deluded I'd been two weeks ago. I'd thought I could have a fling and all my feelings about Tony would go. How naïve.

Still, I held him close and breathed in deeply, savouring his citrus cologne because I wasn't good at being alone.

He broke the kiss and looked into my eyes. 'I have booked a good restaurant in Paddington. I hope you will like it.'

Dave held me back from him, so that he could see what I was wearing.

Perhaps because of my earlier low mood, I was swathed in black. I had on a Diane von Furstenberg wrap dress, which I could wear now that I had dropped a dress size on the love, lust and lies diet.

My cleavage was exposed, but I'd added a lacy black camisole so that if the dress shifted, it didn't show my bra. I'd also put on my favourite Victoria's Secret black, lace-top, thigh-high stockings. Teamed with gold drop earrings and black Manolo Blahnik stilettos on my feet, it was a simple but sexy look.

'Very nice. Very off quickly,' Dave said, mixing his words in his excitement, as he tried to peel the top of my dress aside so that he could see the camisole.

I wiggled out of his grasp though I enjoyed the heat of his

hands on my skin. 'Stop it,' I protested. 'Everyone can see us from the street.'

He looked at his watch. 'Then we go inside before we go to the restaurant. Would you like that Gabrrrriella?' He pressed me against him. 'I'm hungry,' he growled into my ear. 'I want you.'

There was something in Dave's smell, his very potency that still attracted me, but it was in the wrong man. I missed my husband. Yet there was no hope for Tony and me. I had to accept that. I understood the hunger because in that way we were well matched, right from the fateful time Dave walked into my office. Was sex all we had in common? Why couldn't there be more? Lust burned out. Love stayed. I knew that.

'It's good to see you.' I felt so alone with my lies. I wanted Dave's hands on me but for the wrong reason. I wanted to ease the loneliness. I wanted his hot body covering mine. I wanted his thick cock inside of me, so that I could blot out the liar who lived within me. 'Come inside.' I grabbed his hand.

Dave laughed, but his laughter had a growl to it, like a wolf on heat. Not that I picked up the danger signals, the change in attitude that wasn't there before. I didn't think of anything but sex when I was with Dave.

I pulled Dave into my house and straight into the bedroom. The lamp I'd left switched on gave the room a soft welcoming glow. At least this time I had no vision of Tony walking down the aisle of the church to torment me. Nor did I have Cami to worry about.

I bent to undo the delicate straps of my stilettos.

'Leave them on,' Dave ordered. 'Remove the dress.'

I straightened and stared at him. There was a steely edge to his voice. Looking at this six foot four, power-packed lion, I briefly wondered what had got into him.

I reached behind myself and pulled the tie that held my dress together so that the dress came apart. I let it slide off my body.

Dave, who stood in front of me, peeled off his jacket and placed it over my bedroom chair, which sat in the corner. All the while he stared at me, his gaze flicking over me with a raw look of possession in his eyes.

So entranced was I in watching him slowly undo each button of his crisp white shirt that I was aware of my nipples hardening under my bra, and not the change of his mood. I knew he'd have his hands on my breasts soon and his tongue swirling on my nipples before he slid it between my pussy lips. I was so consumed with lust that I didn't pick up that Dave wasn't smiling nor talking, as he usually did.

My gaze roved over him. There was not an ounce of fat on his stomach. His chest was broad like an Olympic swimmer's and his stomach was ridged with muscles so tight that I wanted to run my fingers over the ridges. I couldn't wait to touch him.

He stopped stripping when he got to his trouser button. He flicked it open so that there was just a hint of hair below his navel. 'Do you like what you are seeing?'

'You know I do.'

He pulled off his boots and socks and stood there in his jeans. 'Come here, Gabrrrriella.'

When I walked over to him his arm shot out and he grabbed my wrist, pulling me in fast, so that I nearly stumbled over my stilettos.

I looked at him, alarmed.

He took my hand and ran it over his jean-clad cock. 'Feel how hard I am. This is the effect you have on me. Every time.'

I went to undo his zipper, but his fingers tightened on my wrist. I gasped. I looked into his face.

He frowned at me.

There was a hard glitter in his eyes. I was used to Dave being playful and sexy, even darkly dominant, but not brooding when he was having sex. Since the last time we had been together, something had changed.

Something not good.

'I am furious with you, Gabrrrriella.'

A chill raced up my spine.

'You think of your husband when I am with you.'

'Of course I don't.' Another lie.

Dave gripped my bare shoulders. 'Don't lie to me.'

'Ouch!' I looked over at my shoulder. My skin had turned white around Dave's fingertips. 'Stop that!' I ordered.

I tried to pull out of his grasp but he didn't let me. Instead his mouth came down on mine so swiftly that he bruised my lips. I turned my head away, but he took my face in between his hands and forced me to kiss him.

His kiss was rough and passionate and filled with an animal-like possession. He forced his tongue inside my mouth, filling me with his smell, his taste, his sensuality.

His hands moved to my hair and his fingers scrunched it, so that I couldn't move my face. My hands were butted against his chest.

'I am going to drive that man out of your mind,' he growled.

I raised one eyebrow at him.

Perhaps he disliked my irreverent look, I don't know, but what Dave did next made me take a sharp intake of breath. He picked me up and flipped me over, sat on my bed with me spread across his knee wearing only my lacy stockings, bra and G-string.

With one short sharp motion, he slapped me on the bottom, so that the slap stung where my G-string left my arse exposed.

I yelped. I hadn't been expecting it.

'You wanted me out of here after the wedding.'

'I was tired. It had been a long day.' I tried to turn around to face him but he was having none of it.

A stinging smack came down on my bottom. My skin was so

sensitive I bucked forward to get away from his hand, so that my pelvis pressed into his knee. The pressure gave me a thrill. The trouble was, I was so ready for sex, had been expecting it, that Dave's spanking hurt, but pleasured me too.

'Don't lie to me, Gabrrrriella. I saw Tony come back here, after I left.'

I struggled to get off his knee, but he placed his hand between my shoulder blades and pressed me down.

'Did he fuck you?'

I'd never heard Dave swear before. He was always the perfect gentleman with me. 'Of course not.'

Whack! Down went Dave's hand. 'Did he fuck you?'

'No!'

He smacked me again. I reached around trying to grab his arm but my movements were useless against Dave's strength. I caught a glimpse of his face. There was a wild look in his eyes. Jealous. Possessive.

Dave pinned my hands behind my back and slapped my bottom with his free hand. 'You are mine. Every bit of you is mine.'

My butt stung. My arms ached with struggling, but my pussy was hot. I wanted him to touch me there. I was experiencing such a strange mix of pain and pleasure that I wanted him to turn me over and fuck me hard. I'd never done anything like this before.

I pressed my pelvis into his knee partly to get away from his stinging slaps, partly to get the stimulation of his hard flesh on my mound.

Dave rubbed his hand over my bottom where the skin was pink and tender.

I knew he was punishing me — leaving his mark on me, trying to eradicate Tony from my life.

'Why was that man here?' Dave demanded to know.

'Mind your own damn business.'

Whack!

God this was making me horny. I never knew a spanking could do that.

'I'll make you tell the truth to me, Gabriella. I'll punish you until you do.'

Whack!

Dave had a reason to be angry because my heart still belonged to Tony even though I was tryng to stop thinking about him.

I struggled to get off his knee. 'Stop it, Dave. My bottom is raw,' I cried.

Dave stood and threw me onto the bed. He bent over me and shredded my G-string. I was naked to him. Exposed.

There was a fierce look in his eye. What was he going to do next? The not knowing sent sexual tingles throughout my body.

He knew I'd lied to him, but he couldn't prove it. Dave pressed his hands to my thighs and pushed them wide open so that I was completely vulnerable.

My bottom was stinging against my quilt. I could feel every uncomfortable ridge of the fabric underneath me. I reached up and grabbed his wrists to free myself.

'Don't even bother to struggle, Gabrrrriella, you're going to take everything I do to you tonight. There will be no fast ending like last time. No pushing me out the door so you can bring in your husband. You are going to do exactly what you are told.'

I was enjoying myself and yet, despite my loneliness, I realised that I didn't need Dave. He wasn't a companion in the way that Tony was and he never would be.

Dave leaned between my soft thighs and licked right along my slit up to my clitoris. I groaned and raised my hips to meet his tongue.

Dave circled my clitoris, his tongue hot, wet and pointy. I

was so turned on I could already feel the first little tremors start building inside of me. My clitoris swelled like a marble as he flicked it back and forwards, swirling his tongue around and over the top.

'Oh God, that's good.' I gripped the quilt, arching my hips forward to give him maximum access, and to get some of the pressure off my stinging butt.

Dave was doing it exactly right, the right pressure and the right pace. He knew exactly how to please me. When it came to sex, we were well matched, but that was the only area. That wasn't good enough for me.

When he pushed my vulva upward so that my clitoris was completely exposed and licked me hard, every tingle, every erotic sensation raced along my nerve ends. I was just about to come, savouring the volcanic sensation of approaching orgasm when Dave stopped licking me. He just stopped.

'Keep going,' I cried. I was there. *Right at the climax.* In my desperation, I reached down to rub myself, but Dave grabbed my wrists.

He loomed over me, his eyes narrowed. 'You don't move unless I tell you to.'

'Like hell,' I said, furious that he'd taken the edge off my orgasm–my almost orgasm. 'Since when do you call the shots? I don't have to do a damn thing you say. I'm free now.'

'Is that right, Gabriella?'

I wanted what I wanted and I was perfectly good at pleasuring myself. Given Tony's dud performance over the past three years, I'd become adept at it.

I glared at him and he glared right back. Frustration made me furious. I expected Dave to back off fast, but that was before it had dawned on him that he would have to fight to get my love from Tony.

That knowledge had changed everything.

He climbed off the bed and got to his feet.

I watched him, feeling furious. Dave could be really annoying sometimes. What was he going to do? Leave?

Instead, not taking his gaze off me, Dave unzipped his jeans and slid out of them. He stood at the side of the bed naked, his erection full and heavy.

I wanted him and I'm sure he knew that. Perhaps it was the way my mouth dropped open as I stared at his cock. Dave had a beautiful long, thick cock that he knew how to use.

I hated it that he hadn't let me come. I was so on edge that I knew that having him inside of me would bring me back up to the sexual peak I craved. It's not like I would be able to take out my vibrator in front of Dave tonight. From the look in his eye, he certainly wasn't going to be into any of my games.

Jealousy had made him crazy. In Australia, it's not cool to be jealous. But jealousy is a common emotion in my culture.

Dave walked over to the bed, picked me up and flipped me over onto my stomach without saying a word. I was used to Dave talking, even though it irritated me when he did. I wanted him to talk to me now. I needed something to ease the tension that seemed like static between us.

I didn't like Dave like this, but he took sex to the edge and made me want him.

I turned to look at him standing at the edge of the bed, condom in hand, surveying me like I was his possession. From the expression on his face, Dave was not into talking tonight.

He was into sexual revenge.

Lying on my stomach, my clitoris throbbed, a constant reminder of my dissatisfaction. My pelvis was full and heavy, almost painful. I was still close to coming. It wouldn't take much to bring myself to orgasm and the fact that Dave was determined to sexually torture me infuriated me. I reached down between my legs to stroke myself.

'Don't even think about bringing yourself off,' Dave said. 'You don't move unless I tell you to. I've been too damn nice to you.'

Severely pissed, I started to push myself off the bed, but Dave climbed onto the bed and placed the flat of his palm in the middle of my back and pushed me flat.

Keeping his hand pressed on the flat of my back to keep me still, Dave got behind me, easing his strong thighs between mine. I didn't resist him. I wanted his cock even more than anything.

I was wet so it didn't take much for him to push his cock between my pussy lips. I wanted to say 'about time' but I kept quiet because this damn man was so difficult. For all I knew he could withdraw it and I didn't want that. Oh no! Not when he felt so damned good.

His cock was hot and I clenched my pussy lips around it. I wanted him with a hunger I couldn't explain, but I wasn't proud of that.

Taking my wrists in his hands, Dave lay on top of me, his mouth so close to my ear. 'This is what you need, isn't it? This is *all* you want from me.' His voice was hoarse.

'Yes!'

I could see the pain in his eyes. *How cruel I was.*

He thrust deeply into me. The warm skin of his stomach and thighs grazed my tender bottom. I gasped with pleasure, but I shouldn't have.

I was as cruel to Dave for having sex with him as Tony had been emotionally cruel by not having sex with me.

Dave was right. I didn't love him, even though I wanted to. I loved what he could do to me sexually.

The man could fill me and if I could just wriggle into the right position, I knew I could come. I needed the high that release would bring me. I needed it and it was destroying me.

Dave lay on top of me, dominating me with his weight, but he was the needy one.

He stopped thrusting but I could feel his cock throbbing inside of me.

I arched back, though it was difficult to move. 'Don't stop,' I said.

He released one of my wrists, shifted so that he was on his side and reached around me and stroked my breasts. His fingers were suddenly gentle.

I couldn't believe how sensitive my nipples had become.

Dave thrust into me and he buried his lips into the back of my neck, nipping and kissing the skin so that I squealed with pleasure. I loved what he did to me, especially the way he could touch so many of my erogenous zones like a man possessed.

His hand moved downward between my legs and he stroked me between my legs. It didn't take much, when his fingers hit my clitoris I arched to meet them. I was warm, wet and open. He buried himself deep inside of me, all the while tracing delicious circles around my clitoris.

Perhaps because he hadn't let me come, I don't know, but his possession felt better than it ever had before.

A fiery orgasm hit me, sending rockets off in my head. Dave pinched my nipple with one hand, while thrusting inside of me and stroking my clitoris at the same time.

I didn't have time to draw breath as another wave of orgasms hit me. I ground down hard onto his cock, hearing him growl, feeling his hands clutch my body as he too, came.

Slowly, deliciously, he eased out of me and rolled over onto his back. We both lay apart, not touching or cuddling as we normally did.

Dave didn't say a word.

There was no emotional heat left between us. Perhaps we had burned ourselves out. Perhaps the cruelty of my truth had destroyed it.

I rolled over onto my side and looked at his profile. Dave

remained staring at the ceiling. Normally he would be trying to cuddle me or talking, which irritated me. He lay still. In profile he was as beautiful as a renaissance sculpture, refined and strong, but my heart was cool to him.

I would never fall in love with him. I knew that now. Tony had been my first love, both physically and emotionally. I had thought that love would grow with Dave, as the sex was fantastic. That's how it had been with Tony. Our relationship had started with attraction and grown from lust to love.

I needed to be on my own and for the first time in my life I was ready to be an independent woman.

Dave rolled on his side. I could see unhappiness in his eyes. 'You still love your husband.'

I couldn't lie to him any more. 'Yes. But I'm not having him back.'

Dave dropped his hands from me. 'I can't share your heart. I won't,' he said, his voice choked with emotion. 'I want you to love me.'

This was wrong.

I had to set Dave free.

I gazed at this gorgeous tortured man. 'When I met you in the office that first day, I had no idea things would go this far. My marriage had just broken up, I found you devastatingly handsome. When we went to the Temple, I couldn't say no, but I should have. You see, Dave, I didn't realise that there was such an age difference between us.'

I had no idea that you would want me the way you do.

Dave shrugged. 'I know you're older than me. I know you're in your thirties. I like that about you.'

'I'm forty.'

'Forty?' He stared at me. 'That's not possible.'

'In the restaurant, you assumed I was in my thirties. I didn't correct you. I should have.' I folded my arms tightly in front of myself.

I could see Dave was stunned. His gaze roved over my face and over my body, trying to take it in.

'I'm so sorry, Dave. I know I've hurt you, but you have to understand, I never thought you'd fall in love with me. My husband didn't want me sexually. I couldn't imagine that any man would want me. I...I can't stand lying to you. I can't stand seeing you making plans for a future with me when I know we don't have one.'

I saw him take a deep breath. 'Your age. It doesn't matter.'

I wanted to cry at that moment. Dave had a sweet side that broke my heart. 'I can't have children. I had an emergency hysterectomy when I had Cami. I know you want your own family, with someone who loves you. I'm not that person.'

I saw tears spring to Dave's eyes. He gathered me up in his arms and held me close. His whole body trembled. I could feel his tears falling on my face.

He knew, just as I knew, that we were finished.

I was free.

19

On Sunday morning I went to Mass at Sacred Heart with Cami. As I walked up the aisle, I managed to ignore the querying glances and the blatant stares.

Telling the truth to Dave had given me strength. If I could ask God's forgiveness for my lies, if Dave could forgive me, I could show my face in my community.

I even sat in the same pew as Tony. I realised that somehow we would manage a civilised separation thanks to Tony's good nature. Tony had told me he wanted to make sure that Cami and I stayed in the house and were financially secure. Despite his infidelity, it was impossible to hate him. Somehow my affair with Dave had healed my anger. How could I rail at Tony when I had been with Dave?

I admired his calm the way I had before things went wrong. I was proud of myself too. Proud that I'd found the strength to live my life alone with my little daughter.

While I waited for Mass to start, I studied Tony's features. Tony looked pale. 'How are you feeling now?' I whispered.

'I'm fine,' he said, but he didn't seem it. Call it a woman's intuition. I'd been with him so long that I knew things weren't right.

'You look grey. I think you should go back to the doctor. I think they should run more tests.'

I still loved him, but it didn't eat me up the way it had when we lived together and he didn't want me. Living in separate houses gave me some emotional distance.

Cami looked up at her father's face. She put her hand on his and patted him.

Tony glanced over at his parents, who also shared the pew. 'Shush, Gabby. I'm okay.'

The Mass started, so I turned away from him. Tony's insistence that he was okay left me wondering. He certainly didn't look it, but I didn't feel I had the right to insist he go back to the doctor like I would have once, after all, I wasn't with him any more.

I didn't realise how much I would regret that decision and yet I was proud I'd had the strength to make it.

When I walked into work on Tuesday morning I went straight to Christine's office and knocked on her door.

Christine looked up at me. 'Yes?'

Not good morning, just a blunt yes. I took a deep breath. What I was about to do wasn't going to be easy. My whole body jangled with nerves and a headache had settled across the back of my eyes. 'Can I have a word with you?' I asked.

Christine gave me a sharp nod. Her blonde hair had gel in it and was pulled back behind her ears. Her lips were pinched tightly together, so that they seemed almost white under her pale pink lipstick.

I closed the door behind me and walked over to her desk. As I approached I saw some papers on her desk.

'I have your new work contract here.'

Christine had given it to me to sign a week ago. I saw it needed her signature at the bottom too.

My knees grew weak. I pulled out a chair and sat. 'Before you sign my work contract, I need to tell you something.'

Christine raised a perfectly plucked eyebrow.

'I...I lied to you about Dave Angelo. I did have sex with him. I didn't own up because I was terrified of losing my job. But I don't want you to think that I usually have sex with clients. It was just Dave.'

Christine didn't respond. Instead, she steepled her fingers and rested her chin on her hands.

My stomach churned as I pressed on. 'I...I want to say I'm sorry I let you down. I'd just found out Tony had cheated on me, so I kicked him out. I'm so sorry. I don't know what came over me. I just know that I wasn't thinking straight. I...I think it's because of the turmoil of my marriage breaking up. This isn't the way I normally behave. I've finished it with Dave because I need to learn to be on my own.'

My mouth was dry and I wasn't sure if I was going to be sick. I watched Christine's face waiting to see the disgust register.

She sat back in her chair. 'I know you lied.'

'What?'

Christine turned her computer around and motioned to a file. 'I ordered security recordings from the Temple. They become very interesting when you and Mr Angelo enter the Temple.'

Blood rushed to my head so fast I thought it would explode. 'Th...ey recorded me?' My head spun. I thought I was going to throw up on Christine's spotless beige carpet.

'Gabriella, the Temple has top security. I'm sure you made the security guard's day when you showed Mr Angelo around the Temple's penthouse. I insisted on deleting the original file but I have these copies. I didn't want you to end up on the internet. It would give my agency a bad reputation.'

'Oh my God!'

Christine stood and walked around to my side of the desk, pulled up a chair and sat next to me. I knew she was going to let me go. I mean, I deserved it.

'You must think I'm such a bad person.' *A puttana. Oh God, how did she even want to sit close to me?*

Christine's eyes narrowed as if she was considering what she was about to say. 'In the two years you've worked for me, you've never let me down. I was surprised that you lied to me, but...' Her lips curved slightly. 'I think I would have lied in the same circumstances.'

Had Christine watched those recordings? 'I'll pack my things.'

Christine put her hand on my arm to stop me walking out.

'Gabriella, when I found out my husband was a cheat and my marriage broke up, I screwed everything in trousers for six months. It didn't make me happy, but I did it anyway. I thought it would help me move on. I'm not going to fire you. You're the best damn salesperson I've got. But I think you know that I expect you to keep your sex life out of work hours.'

I couldn't believe it. I swear, I just sat there staring at her. Was she giving me a reprieve? 'Y...you're not firing me?'

'No.'

'Oh, Christine, I don't deserve this. I can't believe you're not going to fire me.' I guess it was the Catholic in me.

I expected a punishment.

'I think if you look up your appointment schedule, you'll see that you have to show clients through the Temple several times today. I'm sure that knowing security will be watching is punishment enough.'

Christine stood. I knew she would feel uncomfortable if I threw my arms around her like I wanted to do for not getting rid of me. She went back to her desk. 'I'm going to sign your work contract. You're a damn good saleswoman, Gabriella. The best I have.'

I stood. 'Thank you.' My mouth was so dry, I'd swear I'd swallowed a handful of sand. My legs were shaking underneath me. I barely knew how I was going to walk out of that room.

'Gabby!'

I looked back at my boss. She pointed to the recordings. 'I'll delete these.'

'Thank you.' How was I going to show clients around the Temple again without wearing a bag on my head? I didn't even want to walk into the place. As it was, I could barely look at Christine.

I made it to the door on wobbly legs.

'You know, Gabby,' Christine said.

I turned to face her.

'I was miserable when my marriage broke up. Utterly devastated. Things got better for me. I established this agency. I met a new man. Things will get better for you, too.'

'Thanks, Christine.' I knew she was trying to help me. I tried to raise a smile. I couldn't, but in my heart I was proud that I had told my boss the truth.

* * *

Three client appointments at the Temple later, with me walking around, head down, trying to do the impossible of avoiding the security cameras. Why hadn't I noticed them before? My mobile phone rang.

When I looked at the caller ID, I saw it was Daniella. Even if I'm in a meeting, I always answer my mother-in-law's calls in case Cami needs me.

'Hello, Daniella,' I said.

'Gabriella, you have to go to North Shore hospital,' said Daniella, her voice trembling. 'Tony's having a heart attack. He's insisting on seeing you.'

'What!' I swear I could hear the blood rushing in my ears.

'Please, Gabriella,' Daniella wailed. 'Be kind to my son. I don't want him to die.'

How did this become my fault? I didn't want Tony to die either.

'I'm coming now,' I said. 'Where are you? Where is Cami?'

'I'm at home with Cami. Pino's left for the hospital. I have to go. I'm trying to get in touch with Dr Amida.'

'Don't do that. Tony won't want Dr Amida,' I protested. Dr Amida, Pino's heart specialist, was not only a good friend of the family but a distant cousin. I suspected that the Italian grapevine was even stronger than doctor confidentiality. Tony wouldn't want his parents to find out about his Viagra overdose.

'Oh my poor son,' Daniella wailed. 'Pino's heart problems started early, too.'

'I've got to go,' I said, snapping my mobile shut.

I apologised to my clients as I hurried them out of the Temple and raced towards George Street where I knew I could hail a cab.

I had to see Tony. What if he died without me by his side?

20

I met Dr Graph at Emergency. His face looked grave and I didn't know what I was going to find. Was Tony dead? Was I too late? My heart was in my mouth. I thought I would faint. I couldn't imagine a world without Tony in it. It wasn't easy to eradicate twenty years.

'Mrs Vitadini,' Dr Graph said.

'How's Tony?' I asked.

'I've stabilised him with nitroglycerin.'

'I have to see him.' I made to move past but Dr Graph held up his hand to stop me.

'Mrs Vitadini, your husband has suffered an angina attack. He — '

'His mother told me a heart attack.'

Dr Graph shook his head. 'Angina is like the first warning of trouble. It's usually caused by reduced blood flow to the heart muscle due to atherosclerosis. It's serious, but not as serious as a heart attack. Now I'll let you see Mr Vitadini on the condition you don't upset him. It's vital your husband remains calm.'

'But I don't understand. Why did you send Tony home? He didn't look well to me. I told you, there's a history of heart trouble in Tony's family.' There had to be more to this than the Viagra.

Dr Graph gave me a look that suggested he didn't appreciate my accusations. 'Mr Vitadini suffered an adverse reaction to Viagra. I took a complete medical history, conducted a physical exam, ordered a chest X-ray and an electrocardiogram. Mr Vitadini's test results showed no plaque build-up.'

Perhaps Dr Graph sensed my inattention because he leaned closer to me. 'What I'm saying to you Mrs Vitadini is that your husband is different from his father.'

'Huh?' What was Dr Graph talking about? 'You mean Tony doesn't have vascular disease like Pino?'

'Angina can also be caused by severe emotional distress.' Dr Graph stared down at me.

'I want to see Tony.'

Dr Graph held up his hands. 'You get ten minutes on the condition that Mr Vitadini remains calm.'

I thought about my behaviour in the emergency room before. Dr Graph had seen me at my worst. There was no getting away from that fact. Somewhat chastened, I walked past him to see Tony.

Tony lay on a gurney, with a white sheet drawn up to his chest. He looked deadly pale. As I walked towards him I had a horrible vision of Dr Graph telling me Tony was dead, of the nursing staff pulling that crisp white sheet over my husband's face, of me leaving the hospital to face Cami, trying to explain to my child that her father was dead.

My stomach clenched with distress. I could taste acid bile in my mouth.

I shook my head, trying to get rid of my fears, but the sombre images were whirling around in my mind.

Beside Tony was a heart monitor making a steady beeping

sound, which was reassuring in one way and terrifying in another.

'I raced here as soon as I heard from your mother,' I said, striding over to him. I sat on the metal chair by the bed and took his hand. Tony's hand was icy in mine. One step from the grave.

'You came,' he said. He gave me a look so searching, so pleased to see me that a lump formed in my throat.

What did he think? That I wouldn't? That I would leave him at the worst time in his life alone? Did he think I would be so cruel? So hard-hearted? What had happened to us?

'Of course I did. But I'm only allowed ten minutes.'

'Don't worry. It's only angina. I'm not going to die,' Tony said.

How typical of Tony to play his condition down. How typical of me to imagine him in the grave. We were so opposite in character in so many ways. Was that why Tony had gone with another woman? Were we too different? Was that why our marriage had fallen apart?

Tony's hand tightened on mine. 'I have to tell you something.' There was a look in his eyes that told me what he had to say was serious.

'You're not to get upset. Dr Graph already thinks I caused this.'

Tony shook his head. He gave me a thin smile. 'You didn't cause any of this. It's my fault. It's always been my fault. I haven't been honest with you.'

I swear the beeping of that heart machine got faster. I shot it a nervous glance. What was Tony about to tell me? Did I want to hear it?

'Don't upset yourself.' I could imagine Dr Graph dragging me out of here, furious with me for stressing his patient.

Tony's hand tightened on mine. 'Shush. Let me speak. You

need to hear this.' He closed his eyes for a moment and took deep breaths. 'I have to talk about Cami's birth.'

Oh my God! Not that. I didn't want to go back to that terrible time. 'Why?' My voice came out in a strangled gasp.

Unbidden, the images flashed in front me. The long agonising labour...Cami stuck in the birth canal with only part of her head showing...the worried face of the doctor...Cami in foetal distress...the doctor rushing me in to surgery...waking up to be told I'd nearly bled to death...that I'd had an emergency hysterectomy...that I'd never have another child...Tony crying by my bedside begging me not to die.

I could feel my own heart thumping. Cami's birth had been the most traumatic time of my life. My only comfort was that Tony had been by my side the whole time. 'I don't think we should talk about that.' I brushed tears from my eyes, but I needed a tissue because my hands were wet with my tears.

Tony squeezed my hand tight. 'Just in case something happens to me, you need to understand why I went with Betty.'

I closed my eyes for a moment. I didn't want to discuss this. Anyway, what did his betrayal have to do with Cami's birth? But Dr Graph had ordered me not to distress him, so I kept my lips pinched shut.

'I saw you suffering. I saw them cut you open. I saw the doctor push Cami's head back inside you.' He shuddered. 'I didn't know if you would survive.' Tony stopped to take a breath. The heart machine started beeping faster.

'Please don't.'

'I wanted to be at your side to help you, but I shouldn't have seen what I did. It stopped me...' He closed his eyes for a moment. His face was pallid. 'What happened to you was my fault. I was selfish. I insisted we try again after the miscarriages, even though you told me your body needed a break. You wanted a rest and you deserved one. I made you pregnant. But I shouldn't have seen what I did,' he repeated. 'It stopped me performing like a man with you.'

I stared into his anguished face as understanding hit me. 'You mean...you mean...you couldn't...make love to me because of what you saw?'

It had never occurred to me that Cami's birth had been as devastating for Tony as it had for me. God knows, I'd ended up in The Clinic.

'The blood.' Tony gripped my hand. 'There was so much blood. On the floor. Everywhere. I thought you were dead. I thought I'd lost you forever. It was my fault.'

Beep, beep, beep went the heart machine, faster than it should be.

Dr Graph's words came back to me. Your husband is different from his father.

Had I got it all wrong? Just as Tony's heart was different from Pino's, was Tony a different type of man?

'Did you have other women before Betty?' I held my breath. I had to hear the truth. I searched his face.

'No. I swear on my life, Gabby.'

I could see the truth in his eyes.

I had assumed he was a philanderer like his father, but he wasn't. He wasn't like that at all. 'You went with Betty to see if you could have sex?'

'I never stopped loving you, Gabby.'

'Why didn't you tell me? We shared all our problems.'

'What? And insult you? Tell you I'd lost my desire?'

'Was that how you felt?' My voice was small.

Tony closed his eyes and shook his head. 'I tried to make love to you, but when I did my head went crazy. I saw the birth...the blood...'

The heart machine beeped alarmingly.

'I've started seeing a counsellor, after the Viagra overdose.'

'But you said those people are crackpots. You refused to go when I suggested counselling.'

'Dr Graph told me to. Gabby, I don't want to lose you. You and Cami are my life.'

Tears were streaming down my face. I thought my own heart would burst. I finally understood why things had gone so wrong for us. I stood, but Tony grabbed my hand, perhaps thinking I was going to walk from that room and leave him forever.

I took a deep breath. The pain of his betrayal still remained. 'I'm glad you shared this with me. I needed to hear the truth, but you should have talked to me a long time ago.'

'Please don't walk out on me, Gabby.'

'You still had sex with another woman, you still betrayed me and that takes some getting used to.'

'And you had Dave,' Tony said. 'I have to accept that, too.'

Tony clutched my hand. 'Come back to me, Gabby.'

The pain in my own chest was unbearable. The heart monitor would be going crazy if I were hooked up to it. 'I made the decision to let you go. You don't know how painful that was for me. I made the decision to be on my own.'

'Please, Gabby. Please forgive me.'

I rubbed the back of his hand with my own, remembering the texture of his skin, remembering the time when we had been so happy together, remembering the love I'd felt for him.'

'I'll try.'

I knew then that things between us could be right again. If Tony could accept that I had a history with Dave, then I could try and accept Betty, now I understood why. It wasn't going to be easy, but we had twenty years of marriage, of love, of joy, of loss. Tony wasn't perfect, but neither was I.

I wanted to save my marriage.

EPILOGUE

Tony, Cami and I took a stroll along Circular Quay from the Opera House to the ferries. It was hot and the sky was a bright blue, the sun having burned off all the morning fog so that I could see the Harbour Bridge clearly. I breathed in the smell of the sea while I admired the boats on the harbour. Tony held my hand. Cami rode her bike in front of us. It felt good, my hand in Tony's. Close. Comforting. Warm.

Like it used to be.

It was six months since Tony's angina attack and he had made a full recovery. I realised how completely contented I was. Much happier than when I'd decided to put myself first.

I had been hard on Tony over his infidelity, but I didn't regret my actions. The funny thing was, Daniella had pulled me aside after our reconciliation, and told me that she wished she'd been tougher on Pino, too.

She told me I did the right thing. Imagine *that* from an Italian mother-in-law.

Even Bisnonna welcomed me into the family, which meant she must have lifted her curse. At least, I assumed she did because my life had changed for the better. I think it was because she thought that now I was with Tony, that left Dave free for her. She asked me for his phone number but I told her I'd deleted it from my mobile phone.

Tony and I had been to plenty of counselling together. The counsellor told us that Tony had post-traumatic shock, which explained why he kept reliving Cami's terrifying birth. With counselling, talk and patience it was treatable.

Tony slid his arm around my waist and suddenly pulled me to him, kissing me with passion. 'I love this place,' he said. 'It reminds me of when we were dating.'

I ran my fingers through his hair. 'I love you,' I said simply. We were pressed together pelvis to pelvis. I liked it when Tony held me like this. I could feel the heat of him through his jeans. A silent understanding passed between us. If we tired Cami out enough, she might have a sleep in the afternoon, which left it free for all the pleasurable things we could do to each other.

With no recriminations and no anger between us, Tony had recovered to the sexy, exciting man he had been before we had Cami.

'Cami wants to go on a ferry ride. Should I get her to pedal really fast, while I run alongside her?' Tony asked. He raised his eyebrows. 'We have to tire her out somehow.'

I laughed. He was cute, my husband. I was so glad to have him back in my life. 'Go ahead. Do your best,' I called out after him.

I watched as he challenged Cami to a race. She pedalled as fast as her three-year-old legs could manage. I smiled as Tony let her get ahead of him.

As I walked, I noticed a black Porsche drive along beside me. I looked in the window. The driver was talking animatedly to his sleek, brunette passenger. It was Dave and Vanessa Boyd.

I'd heard that Mr Boyd had passed away. Vanessa had a big smile on her face as she looked at Dave. I watched the car as it passed by me. Dave was so busy talking he hadn't seen me, but I'm sure if he had, he would have waved.

I was happy for Dave. Vanessa would enjoy all the passion he had to give.

As for me, I can't say I regretted the affair. I regretted not being honest about my age with Dave in the first place, but clearly that hadn't bothered him the way I thought it would. I regretted that Tony hadn't talked to me about his problem because I would have done anything to help him. All I knew was thanks to Dave, my husband became so jealous he fought to get me back and that made me feel loved.

It was exactly what I needed.

Thanks for reading *Love Lust and Lies*. I hope you enjoyed it.

If you'd like to know more about me, my books, or to connect with me online, you can visit my webpage cathleenross.com, follow me on Twitter @cathleenross, or like my Facebook page

http://www.facebook.com/cathleen.ross.3

If you enjoyed this book, please leave a review. Reviews can help readers find books, and I am grateful for all honest reviews. Thank you for taking the time to let others know what you've read, and what you thought.

www.ingramcontent.com/pod-product-compliance
Lightning Source LLC
LaVergne TN
LVHW041209150826
845673LV00001B/335

* 9 7 9 8 6 9 5 9 1 8 8 0 9 *